Bossy Billionaire

A Hate To Love WorkPlace Billionaire Romance

Cocky Billionaire Boys
Book 2

Chiquita Dennie

304 Publishing Company

Latest Releases

Series

Struck in Love

The Early Years-A Prequel Short Story
Ruthless:Antonio and Sabrina Book 1
Savage: Antonio and Sabrina Book 2
Beast: Antonio and Sabrina Book 3
Captivated By His Love:Janice and Carlo
Brutal: Antonio and Sabrina Booke 4
Redemption: Antonio and Sabrina Book 5

Heart of Stone

Broken, Book 1 (Emery & Jackson)
A Valentine's Day Short Book 1.5 Emery & Jackson
Rebirth, Book 2 (Jordan and Damon)
Reveal, Book 3 (Angela and Brent)
Bottoms Up Book 3.5 Jessica and Joseph Short
Renew, Book 4 (Jessica and Joseph)

Cocky Billionaire Boys

Cocky Catcher (Cocky Billionaire Boys Book 1)
Bossy Billionaire (Cocky Billionaire Boys Book 2)

<u>The Fuertes Cartel</u>

Stolen (The Fuertes Cartel Book 1)

Saved (The Fuertes Cartel Book 2)

Betrayed (The Fuertes Cartel Book 3)

<u>Carrington Cartel</u>

Torn: The Carrington Cartel Book 1

Claim: The Carrington Cartel Book 2

<u>Something</u>

Something Gained: A Romantic Comedy Book 1

Something Earned: A Romantic Comedy Book 2

<u>Pierce Motors</u>

Refuel: (Pierce Motors Book 1)

Pressure: Pierce Motors Book 2)

<u>Summer Break</u>

Summer Nights: (Summer Break Book 1)

<u>TN Seal Security</u>

Aydin: Book 1

Nasir: Book 2

Nicco: Book 3

<u>Standalones</u>

Until Serena(HEA World Novel)

Temptation

She's All I Need

I Deserve His Love

Mutual Agreement

Scoring with Sadie

Exposed (A Bodyguard Novel)

Love Shorts:A Collection of Short Stories

Red Light District(A Fantasy Romance Short)

For my Family

I want to dedicate this book to my family and friends. You're always with me no matter where I go and everything you've taught me has made me a better person.

Introduction

Are you signed up for my newsletter?

Join today and find out all the latest in new releases, contests, giveaways, sneak peeks and more.

www.chiquitadennie.com

Author Inspiration

"Never allow anyone to steal your joy. It doesn't matter how many times someone says you can't do something. Invest in yourself—even if it's just writing down what your goals and plans are. Starting small can lead to bigger things."

—Chiquita Dennie

Disclaimer

This work of fiction contains strong language and explicit sexual content and is only intended for mature readers. This story may contain unconventional situations, language, and sexual encounters that may offend some readers. If you're looking for sweet, fluffy romance, I would recommend another book. This book is for mature readers (18+).

Character Interview: Ethan West

Ladies and gentlemen, we have the major banking billionaire, and potential governor of New York, Ethan West, sitting with us today. We're discussing his journey in the latest release from author Chiquita Dennie. Welcome to our sixth installment of interviewing our characters. We look forward to many more and love hearing your questions.

Interviewer: So happy you've joined us today. I know you're a busy man so I'll get right into the questions so readers can start reading about your journey. How do you feel about your story being told?

Ethan: First, I want to say thank you to the author and the readers for letting me take up a little time from your day to send in questions. After working things out with Gage, I was advised to reach out to the author about having my story told and what my plans are for the future. Now we have this new release coming.

Interviewer: How did Nina become attached to your campaign? We've seen her in a few shots at your campaign stops.

Ethan: I met Nina through Gage as business associates in banking and he invited me to his fundraiser many years ago and we had mutual friends with Gage. Nina was kind enough to help me with doing small town halls at her community center.

Interviewer: What would you say is the good and bad of running for governor?

Ethan: I can't spoil anything, but I would say the good is that I get to connect with people I normally wouldn't see while I'm stuck in a stuffy office. The bad is dealing with corrupt politicians and the media trying to make me out to be something I'm not.

Interviewer: So, are you saying working with your fellow politicians would be difficult?

Ethan: I'm saying that for me to get anything done I need to figure out the best way to work with everyone's ego that represents every constituent in New York.

Interviewer: I hear you're getting your cousin to take over West Banking and Investments?

Ethan: I am, he's proven himself and I want to make sure no conflicts are brought up with me and my business, so I've assigned him to take over as CEO.

Interviewer: Was it love at first sight?

Ethan: We're talking about Maya Armstrong? That woman drove me crazy.

Interviewer: For readers that want to know if you've found love in this story, can you give us a hint?

Ethan: I'm a bachelor, always have been. I can say some people come into your life for a reason.

Interviewer: Can you give us more details on your plans for governor, since we can't get any hints on your love life?

Ethan: I'm looking to make the government work for all people and not just the people at the top. I want the citizens of New York to vote based on my ideas and not who I'm sleeping with.

Interviewer: Can you give us one spoiler?

Ethan: I think I can tell you that Maya is still the same crazy, sassy woman you met in Nina and Gage's story. She's met her match with me.

Interviewer: Tell us your favorite politician besides yourself?

Ethan: Easy. President Lincoln. He went against party to do what's best for the country and not for himself.

Interviewer: I know I speak for all the readers today when I say that we appreciate you for hanging with us today. Readers enjoy and let us know how Ethan fairs in this new release.

Synopsis

He never expected to justify himself to anyone, least of all a celebrity talk-show host.

Ethan West has been in the political race long enough to know how to play the game. Shine a light on your good deeds and keep your playboy ways in the dark. As a man of few words, he doesn't answer to anyone, instead demands answers from those running against him. When an ex-lover reveals his playboy lifestyle to the press, Ethan accepts an interview with Maya Armstrong, to save his political aspirations.

Maya Armstrong is known throughout the industry as headstrong, fearless, and independent. When Ethan takes a seat on her couch, she's determined to hold this billion-aire banker turned politician accountable for his actions. The last thing she expected was for the sparks to fly on and off air.

Find out what happens when two alpha personalities collide. Will this rift end his

campaign, or will it be the beginning of something much more lasting, like love?

Chapter 1

Maya

It all started seven months ago when I met *him*. It was at Genesis J. Maguire's fundraiser bachelor auction that our mutual friends, Genesis and Scottie, threw every year to raise money for various charities. I didn't like his straitlaced, cocky, alpha attitude, and he didn't like my cocky, alpha, headstrong attitude, so imagine my surprise when we ended up in bed together.

Afterward, he started to come around more because of his growing friendship with Nina and Gage. Gage was Nina's husband, and the father of her twins. I loved their relationship. They started off rocky at first, but now I looked at them as the perfect couple—even if they didn't think they were. One day, I wanted to get married and have kids, too—*if* I could find a guy who had a job, didn't live with his mom, and wouldn't cheat on me, but who *would* spoil me rotten and give me sex at least three times a day.

That man definitely wasn't *him*. Even though I decided to try not to come across as uptight any more for the sake of his friendship with Nina and Gage, a few times, I could admit that I was pissed he didn't remember me from the one night we'd spent together. Even though my attitude was always sex and no love, for a grown man not to remember having the best sex of his life with *Maya Armstrong* was a bruise to my ego.

So here I was sitting in a car creeping outside his place of business to see if he was dating someone. The media kept him in the press and blogs with multiple women every other day and a part of me wanted to turn into the crazy girlfriend, *but I shouldn't be jealous right?* He and Nina ended up becoming friends and coming around more. I chuckled to myself sitting in the car with my binoculars scoping out the scene.

"Did you bring the barbecue Pringles this time?" Scottie remarked, looking through the clear bag holding our snacks.

I nodded at the second bag I had in the back. "Where did you tell Genesis you were going tonight?" I asked, checking the time on my watch.

For the past few weeks, he'd been working late at the office until nine at night. He was still helping his friend in the primary stage of his campaign, and the first focus group he'd pulled together ended two hours ago. Yeah, that was right; I was following Ethan "Billionaire Banker" West, of the super-wealthy, upper-crust West family, who had their names on all the financial buildings and hotels in New York. He was a trust-fund baby, but he made his billions from investments and bonds, opening a chain of banks named after his family. By the time he turned twenty-eight, he was a billionaire, and now at thirty-two, he'd thrown his name in the ring to run as an Independent candidate for the next governor of New York.

I turned to look at Scottie as she giggled in the driver's

seat. I peeked over her shoulder and noticed she was texting. She showed me her text exchange and I shook my head laughing.

"He told me to bring him some food if we're not out too late on our 'Mission Impossible' task," Scottie said, laughing, showing the text from Genesis.

I shook my head at them. "What made you pursue things with Genesis?" I asked, curious. "I mean, Ethan's a very wealthy and high-profile man, just like Gage and Nina. I don't know if I should continue with my 'Mission-Impossible' task, as Genesis would call it," I said cautiously, sighing.

"He didn't give up."

"Who?" I asked.

"Genesis. Even when I tried to push him away, he didn't give up on our relationship, just like Nina and Gage. You know what happened with them, and the conflict with his family. He continued to fight for her, and Nina realized that she loved him more than the mistake he made. Same with Genesis and me. You have to ask yourself, is he worth the ride or not?" Scottie replied, pointing to the office building in front of us.

A knock on my window startled us both. A pizza delivery guy stood at my window. The weird thing is that neither of us ordered food, but my stomach was grumbling. I looked at her and she shrugged her shoulders nonchalantly. I rolled the window down to see what he wanted.

"Yes?" I asked, nervously looking around the parking lot.

He pulled the pizza out of the heating case and tried to pass it to me. I tried to turn it away and he insisted.

"This is for you, ma'am," the delivery guy said.

Scottie started to pull money out of her purse. "What are you doing?" I questioned.

"Paying for the pizza. I don't know about you, but I'm starving."

"Sir, we didn't order this. I think you have the wrong person," I told him.

He looked at the receipt and looked back up at me right as the front door of the office opened and *he* appeared, talking on his cell phone, and winking right at me. I thought all this time he didn't know I was out here, but maybe we weren't as discreet as I thought.

"That gentleman right there wearing the suit told me to give this to you and to say, 'see you tomorrow night'," the delivery guy said as he quoted the words from his notepad as a large lump formed in my throat.

Five months earlier

Once Nina introduced me to Scottie and Diya, we became close friends. Scottie was the one I called on when I desired to do something unorthodox, or I called for advice, since she had online blog and radio show the *Scottie's* Hour. Seeing the things that she had to answer made me question other people's mindsets on dating; you'd never catch Maya Armstrong going overboard to get a guy's attention! Nina was the mom of the group; she would talk you out of whatever you were thinking of doing. Diya was a mixture of them both; you could call her to bail you out of jail, but she'd give you a lecture about why you ended up in jail on the car ride home.

Nicole was Nina's sister, and the youngest in our group. She was still finding herself. She'd stopped working at the community center and started working at a sex shop, and on the weekends, she could be seen as DJ Nic at a club in Brooklyn. She was into techno music now, wearing a short bob wig and dating different guys.

I tended to call Scottie more than Nina because Nina had a lot on her plate with being married, having three kids, and working at the community center. It was flourishing, now that they got the funding situation fixed. Gage was home with the twins and Tailynn this morning. He was still on contract with the Raptors, and, after winning the World Series, things got even crazier for him. He was taking on more TV opportunities and movies. As I got older, I admired their relationship more and more every day. I was proud of my friend for not giving up on love.

I, on the other hand, didn't believe in the happily-ever-after. I dated strictly for my own pleasure; the only things men were good for were taking me on trips and giving me mind-blowing orgasms.

Was my heart closed off to love? Yep. Did a guy break my heart? Yep. I learned two definite things in life; you're born, and then you die. The in-between was a matter of how you wanted to spend your moments and with whom. So, the second I walked in on my boyfriend having sex with another woman, I cut off opening my heart to anyone. He apologized and thought buying me things would make up for his cheating, but I stood strong and cut him off. His excuse was that I was too hard and emotionally unavailable. It made me question everything about myself, and I ended up realizing that I was projecting my parents' situation onto all the relationships in my life.

Plus, I was building my career. Did I work a lot? Hell

yeah. I was trying to make it in the entertainment industry as a TV host personality. That business was hard and being nice and letting people walk all over you wouldn't cut it if you wanted to become the next in-demand host. *Spotlight with Maya* was on basic cable, on Channel 10, the FBX network. I'd started out with a blog called *Spotlight with Maya* and moved into TV after the FBX president's daughter found my blog and posts on celebrity news and gossip. On top of that, I was really into social media; I had five-hundred thousand followers, and brands wanted me to post their products and fashion styles, so I proposed turning my blog into a TV show, and now I was a local celebrity.

I was on my way to hang out with the girls at the gym. When I got there, Scottie and Nicole were on the elliptical machines. I went off to work on my legs. Staying toned and healthy was my goal, since I was on TV and in the public eye.

Nina picked up the towel off the elliptical machine, wiping the sweat off. "I need to lose another ten pounds, and then I'll be ready for the fundraiser this year. Scottie, is Genesis doing another Bachelor and Bachelorette theme?" Nina asked, changing the timer to low for cooldown.

Scottie was nodding her head.

"How are the twins doing?" I questioned. I loved those babies. Spoiling them was my passion, even if I had to fight Nina to do it. Nina hated it when I spoiled Tailynn with a girls' day and she came back constantly talking about buying Gucci or Fenty beauty.

"Kids are good. Even with all the crap you buy them that they're not old enough to play with. I think it's too late for Tailynn; she can't be saved. Gage said we should ground her for the next twenty years because she's turning into another you." Nina cackled as I glared at her.

"Genesis said the same thing about Celine," Scottie commented, stepping off the machine and taking a sip of water. "Whatever you're doing to the girls, they're becoming more and more into fashion and makeup. The other day, Celine said, 'you're very last year'." She narrowed her eyes at me. "Shocked wasn't the word. And she walked away, FaceTiming with Tailynn. Genesis sat there, laughing at me—until I threw a pillow at him."

I wiped the sweat off my brow. I raised my water bottle to my lips, remembering how hardhearted I'd been toward relationships, and how I didn't really give men a chance when it came to commitment. I grew up with a father who focused his life on pleasing my mother, only to have her cheat on him with a co-worker, and he still forgave her. To this day, I had a weird bond with her because out of that relationship came a child, so we were raised together. Kasey Hughes, a twenty-six-year-old librarian. Over time, we became close, and we had our moments because she barely got along with our mom. The woman was straight selfish. The problem was that I took after her in looks. I was five-five and a curvy one-hundred and forty-five pounds, with sharp cheekbones, full lips, and smooth, chestnut-brown skin. I took after her in personality, too—except I did care about people, unlike her.

Still, my parents, Michael and Hazel Armstrong, demanded that we all have Sunday dinner every week together—which meant I needed to prepare myself to try to be the perfect daughter.

"What was the question that pertained to you getting schooled?" Nina inquired.

"She was talking about the lip gloss colors, and I said my clear lip gloss—that I've had for seven months now, mind you—was cute, and she looked at me, shaking her head," Scottie said, impersonating Celine.

All three of us burst into laughter as she pretended to hold up a phone and nonchalantly walk off.

"Leave my babies alone and tell Gage and Genesis not to hate the fabulousness that I bring to my nieces' lives," I remarked, putting a hand on my hip, and rolling my eyes with a grin.

"Now they're your nieces, but when we ask you to babysit, we never hear from you," Scottie teased, tilting her head, and folding her arms across her chest.

The three of us stood silently, and then burst into laughter when a guy walked into the room, looking at all three of us and licking his lips. They both shouted, "Married!" and I bent over in laughter, clapping my hands together.

Nina and Scottie and I walked over to the front facing mirrors of the private VIP room, stretching to prepare before lifting weights. "Is Kasey going to your moms for Sunday dinner?" Nina asked, folding her arms behind her head, stretching.

I tightened my ponytail. "Last time I talked with her she wasn't. But who knows? She stays in her romance books. You can't get her out for nothing."

"I wanted to formally invite you ladies to the upcoming fundraiser that Genesis's company is throwing. Maya, maybe you should invite Kasey to come with you," Scottie murmured, standing up from tying her shoes.

"Scottie, I was going to ask you about your friend, Ethan. I've heard some rumors he's running for governor of New York?" I remarked, changing the subject from my family.

"I heard those rumors, too; he didn't tell me anything about it when we talked the other day," Nina stated, dropping the dumbbell onto the mat.

"I want an interview with him. Not like the one I did with Gage. No offense, Nina."

"Yeah. I remember that. How is your show doing?" Nina asked, irritated at the episode I did with Gage a year ago.

I planted my hands on the floor in a downward dog, stretching my left leg, and then my right leg before doing push-ups. "The ratings aren't the greatest, not like they used to be. But I trust that my audience is loyal and will stick with me."

"I can talk with him and see; I can't promise, though. He's extremely busy, and if his campaign kicks off, I doubt he could ignore a sit-down with you, since you're popular and have the ear of the young people," Scottie admitted.

"Thanks friend," I commented.

"Can we go? I'm tired and hungry. I need a bath and wine," I complained, rolling the yoga mat up.

"We can head to my house. I know Gage is going crazy with the kids, probably," Nina said.

Chapter 2

Ethan

I was waiting in front of one of my branch manager's desks at the Manhattan office, looking over the numbers for a loan that Richard approved. The client wasn't returning his calls. He sat, wiping the sweat off his face.

"Richard, I don't care what he says; I have the contract he signed in front of me. I propose you do your job and make sure he understands that Ethan West doesn't play by someone else's rules."

"Sir, I understand, but he recently closed his offices and left the state."

With a furrowed brow, I asked, "And how is that my problem? I've repeatedly told you that no loans should be approved out of this branch without my sign-off. That was after your last screw-up with the Walters Shipping Company that cost me one-point-two million dollars."

A knock at the door interrupted us, and Hannah, my ex-girlfriend, walked inside. "Ethan, they told me I'd find you here." She greeted me with a relieved smile. "How are you?"

"Hannah. I don't have time for this, I'm in the middle of a meeting." I was shocked and annoyed to see her.

I hadn't seen her in over two years. She was too obsessed with wanting to be married and have kids, but her selfishness, narcissistic attitude, and jealousy drove me to end things. Hannah had everyone thinking we'd be married with kids and I hadn't even been with her a year. My parents loved her because they're friends with her parents. Knowing I was ending things, she tried to fake a pregnancy to get me to stay. Then the nail in the coffin was her sleeping with one of her clients, some B-list movie star her company represented.

She slid in closer and ran a hand up my chest, tapping the bridge of my nose. Hannah was the type that couldn't understand that no meant no. She's a publicist for a magazine.

Richard cleared his throat. "Uhm, Ethan, I have a meeting with Hannah."

"Meeting about what?"

"I'm having some of my clients move their banking to your branch. I know how you do business and I still have my money here, so I thought this would be a good reconnection."

"Richard, leave."

"But I..."

I glared at him. This was not the time for him to question me. Slipping my hands in my pockets, I stood in front of her as she tried to sexily reach up and kiss me on the cheek. I took a step back, blocking her kiss.

"You look intense, Ethan, maybe you need me to help you relax."

"What I need is for you to leave me the hell alone.

Remove your money from my bank and forget you ever met me."

She walked over and sat on the top of the desk, crossing her leg.

"No."

"No?"

"Yeah, no. I apologize for how things went between us, but you *made* me behave that way with your long work hours and fooling around on me."

"I never cheated on you, and if I recall, we had an open relationship—something that *you* wanted. The rule was to not be with anyone you work with or any of the other person's family members. But you let me think you were pregnant when I told you I didn't want kids, and you went behind my back to manipulate my parents."

Richard knocked on the door and poked his head back inside.

"Richard, remove Hannah's account from this branch and see that she no longer has access to any of my branches. Get the word out to all managers."

"You can't do that!" she squealed.

"Sir, don't you think that's a little drastic?" Richard responded, walking inside as Hannah got off my desk.

"Are you sleeping with Hannah? If you are, I recommend you stop and get tested."

"Ethan!"

"Do what I say, Richard. Get my money back and close her account. That Lawrence deal was your mishandling, and it cost me more money with this college fraud scheme. If you don't want to lose your job, you better have good news for me within the next twenty-four hours." I walked out, ignoring Hannah, who was still screaming my name.

Getting inside of the limo, I checked my phone for any messages. Just a message from Genesis to meet him at his office.

"Walter, can you head over to Genesis Holdings Inc.?"

"Yes, sir." He turned around at fifth and Manhattan, heading to the Upper East Side. Thirty minutes later, he pulled up to the front door of Genesis's office, and I opened the door before he could.

I didn't need a badge to get upstairs because everyone knew Genesis and I went back a few years. I hopped on the elevator toward his private office as the doors opened to his assistant, on the phone, waving for me to go inside.

I tapped on the door.

"Ethan West, how are you?" Genesis stood up from his desk, reaching out to shake my hand.

"Something must really be on fire for you to text me during the middle of the day to come meet you as soon as possible."

His smile was without humor. "I have a source that tells me that your ex, Hannah, is up to something that could potentially harm your campaign if you decide to run." He motioned for me to sit down.

"Hannah isn't stupid."

"I'd like to believe you, but if you're planning on running for governor, then you need to find out what she wants and give it to her."

"She wants to get back together and that's not happening."

"I can understand, but are you serious about being the next governor of New York?"

"I can tell you that I'm leaning closer to having an answer, just wrapping things up with the company.

Richard made some bad deals and now it has my name in potentially bad press articles."

"They say bad press can be good press. Do you need help?"

"I have it under control right now. Hannah, I'm not really worried about her."

"Okay, if you think so."

"Who's the source?"

"If I tell you, it won't be a source anymore."

* * *

The next day, I was sitting at home, eating breakfast that Athena cooked for me. Athena had worked as my house-keeper for the past five years. At sixty-seven, she still liked to hang out with her friends and gamble—even though if you let her tell it, she was not a day over thirty-five. She didn't clean, hated doing windows, and gave me attitude when I came home late at night sometimes. Anyone would probably wonder why I kept her around. But she was like a second mother to me—one who held me accountable and told me when I was doing wrong. I tried to tell her to let me spoil her and not to do so much because of her bad leg, but she refused to relax.

I started to open the paper when my phone rang. My mother's name was on the screen.

Throughout my life, my parents, Lucy and Henry West, had tried their best to control me. We came from money, and what people didn't know was that at one point, my family almost went broke—until I helped bail them out. My father had a problem with bad investments and gambling. Throughout my life, he was either up or down with his money. That money came from his grandfather, and he built our family wealth—until the stock market crash in 2008.

I was smart enough to keep my trust fund from my grandfather, invest it, and make it work for me. I took my inheritance, invested it in bonds, stocks, and offshore investments, and worked it to the point of becoming a millionaire. "Ethan West, what the hell is going on!" my mother, Lucy, screamed over the phone. I opened the paper, sipping my coffee as Athena went to place my plate of food on the table.

"Oh, my," Athena said, dropping the plate on the floor instead.

"What are you talking about, Mom?"

"Have you not seen the newspapers? Talk to your son, Henry, because I cannot deal with this."

"When did you get engaged, son?"

I spit the coffee I had just taken a sip of out at his statement. "I'm not engaged."

Now, at thirty-two, I was a billionaire. I had branches all over the country, and I could say my reputation of being bossy and arrogant was, to an extent, true. But the only way to get to the top was to make sure my business flourished. I had people depending on me—not only my family, but employees around the world. And now, I was focused on my next goal: potentially becoming the next governor of New York. There was certainly no time in my life for a long-term relationship, especially not one that involved me getting engaged.

"Are you reading the paper?" he asked.

My phone started beeping that I had another call.

"I am."

"Turn to the Entertainment section."

I placed the phone down on the table so I could flip

through the sections. I found the front page showcasing a large photo of Hannah and I holding hands with a quote saying we were in love.

"I'm going to kill her."

"Son, you're not thinking clearly. This is a good thing; it just wasn't done the right way. Your poor mother is over here crying because you left her out of the loop."

"I'm not engaged."

"You should be, and you should have kids by now, Ethan. You're 32 years old."

"I'll call you back."

"No, you will not. I'm calling Hannah to set up a lunch date for our families to meet."

"Lucy, do you hear yourself? There is no wedding."

"Ethan, I am your mother and you will not speak to me that way. Hannah apologized for her mistakes so it's time to forgive and move on. Henry, do you hear this?"

"The girl is crazy!" I spat, jumping up out of my seat and taking the other paper out of Athena's hands and tossing it into the trash. "Listen I have to go and take care of some things. I'll call you later," I said, hanging up not waiting for them to answer.

"I told you she was a crazy nut."

"Athena, please don't start."

She stood and took my new plate of breakfast along with hers and tossed the food away. I'd lost my appetite.

"What? I advised you a long time ago to let that girl go. She's bad news and you listened to your mother and she ain't right in the head either."

"Athena."

"What? Hannah is the last person you should go back to dating. Shit, all those nights I heard her screaming when y'all were having sex. Sounded like a damn banshee."

"Woman, are you eavesdropping on me?"

"Boy, don't flatter yourself with that little pickle you got. It's called overcompensating because she wants the money. Now get out there and fix this mess. I can't stand having all those paparazzi hanging around in the bushes," she said, cupping my chin and smiling.

"I know you're right. I already have Richard's fuck up to deal with and now Hannah's psycho ass."

Athena walked off shaking her head yelling over her shoulder. "Fire him."

I stalked toward my bedroom. I dropped my phone on my bed and changed my clothes. I buttoned up my jacket, grabbed my keys off the dresser, and left out toward my car. I wasn't taking a driver today. Walter had a family and I wasn't planning on being long.

Leaving my gated home, I drove off toward the highway and headed to Hannah's place.

Forty minutes later, I pulled up to her home at Dame Tower and left my keys with the valet. Not waiting for the elevator, I walked up the stairs and knocked on her door. I heard giggling on the other side. I clenched my fists, knowing she was probably plotting right now, after that fake story. Hannah was determined to draw me back in, but I refused. She could play all the games she wanted. It was only making her look crazy.

"Ethan, what a pleasant surprise." Hannah held the door closed keeping me from looking inside.

"Have you lost your mind?" I pushed my way inside, looking around at clothes and lingerie on the couch and floor.

"What are you talking about?"

"Engaged?"

She shut the door and sauntered up close to me, running her hand up my chest, trying to wrap her arms around my neck.

I moved out of her embrace.

"Ethan!" Richard screeched, trotting out of the room in his underwear and the newspaper.

"Richard."

"It's not what you think," Hannah said.

"Hannah, I don't care who you sleep with; the problem is the lie you're telling the public. We broke up because you cheated on me, and I haven't looked back ever since. Leave me alone and put out a statement that this engagement is a lie. I can promise you that you don't want to push me."

"I didn't put the story out and what's so wrong about getting back together? I've changed. Richard doesn't mean anything to me," Hannah answered, a stern expression in place.

"We're done here. Richard, I suggest you clean out your office because the next time I see you, it will be from behind a jail cell for fucking up my business."

Chapter 3

Ethan

The next day, after I finished checking up on all my banks, I went home and changed into a pair of jeans, a black t-shirt, and Jordans. It was rare that I wasn't wearing a suit all hours of the day with the way my schedule went, but I usually dressed casual on the weekend for hanging out with my friends and family —and sometimes, my female companions.

The tattoo shop was bustling with loud laughs, music, and neighbors hanging out, even though they weren't getting tattoos. Since Gage and I worked out our differences, we'd become friends again, and he'd introduced me to his friends, Talbot and Diya. I was already familiar with Genesis from running in the same circles in the business industry.

Talbot stopped working the needle gun on Gage and looked up at me. "Gage was telling me you're thinking of running for governor of New York, Ethan?"

I ran a hand down my face. "It's a possibility. I'm still exploring my options, and the amount of time it would take on a campaign trail."

"His ass is running; don't let him fool you," Gage explained, sitting up. "He's one of those politicians who can sell you anything. What ticket and platform are you running on? I know your family donates a lot to Republican politicians."

"It may surprise you, but I'm an Independent and think for myself. I love my family, and they have their beliefs, same as I have mine. You know something about that, don't you, Gage?" I remarked, furrowing my brows, then stopped to take a picture with a woman who was nonstop flirting with me as she waited for her friend to finish up her tattoo.

"So, if you run for governor of New York, you're going to need a First Lady, right?" the young woman seductively asked, running a hand up my chest.

I stared at her fingers, smirking.

"Ethan, how are you? I haven't seen you in the bank in a while," Diya said. She and Talbot had moved their business banking to West Bank a month earlier.

I reached out and hugged Diya back. "I'm fine, Diya. How are you doing with this one here?" I asked, pointing at Talbot.

She hugged him from behind, kissing him on the cheek. "He's not so bad. And if I can throw my two cents in on the debate, you should really think about running for governor, Ethan," Diya said, striding over to the receptionist's desk. She rang up another customer who had just finished getting a tattoo of a dragon on his arm.

I had a few tattoos on both arms: one of my last name; the second one of my mother's name; and the third one was my housekeeper Athena's name.

Talbot wiped his station down and Gage stood to

walk over and pay. "How many more tattoos are you planning on getting?" Talbot asked Gage.

He shrugged in answer. "What are you about to do now, Ethan? Talbot and I are headed to go play a round on the field. You interested in getting your clean clothes dirty?" Gage questioned.

"Sure, I have a little time before I meet with my campaign manager," I responded.

"Who's your campaign manager?" Gage inquired, walking out of the shop with me strolling beside him.

"I hired Tim Richards to help me explore a possible run. He's won multiple campaigns and I think he's good."

"Talk with Genesis. He can probably give you some insight into Tim. What about doing a few small, informal questions with Scottie on "Scottie's Hour" radio and blog. That way, you can test the waters. See if this is something you want to do and get a feel for things before going through the real thing on a long, drawn-out campaign," Gage suggested, opening the driver's side door.

I went to my Range Rover and followed him. He took off into traffic, driving his Camaro, not paying attention to me following him as he weaved in and out of traffic. Ten minutes later, we pulled up to his massive home that he'd had built for his family. Stepping out of my car, I followed him to the door as the twins and Tailynn came running and scrambling to hug him.

"Daddy! Daddy!" all three screamed.

He bent down to pick Thalia up and pulled Tailynn into his side while walking toward the living room. "Where's Mommy at, girls?" Gage wondered, kissing the top of Thalia's forehead. She snuggled in his arms with her little doll.

"She's in the kitchen," Tailynn said, sitting next to him on the couch.

"Everyone, say hi to Mr. Ethan. He's a friend of daddy's," Gage told them.

I smiled and waved. Tailynn waved back and Thalia grinned.

"What's going on in here?" Nina came into the room wiping her hands on a towel.

"Mommy, look at my dolly," Thalia said holding her Cabbage Patch doll out to Nina.

Gage stood with Thalia in his arms and walked over to Nina and pulled her into his arms, kissing her on the lips deeply.

"Can you guys wait to do that when we're not here? That's gross." Tailynn motioned like she was throwing up.

I chuckled at her response.

"Nina, how many turnips did you put in this smoothie? I need a glass of wine because this damn green smoothie is not working for me. I might as well eat dirt."

A woman walked into the room wearing a cut-out strappy bra and short biker shorts. The curves of her hips in the shorts and her toned abs and arms caused me to stare.

"My eyes are up here, buddy boy!" She snapped her fingers, pulling me out of my trance.

Nina and Gage looked over at me.

I cleared my throat. "Sorry. I'm Ethan West, and you are?" I reached a hand out to shake hers and she ignored it. "Do we know each other?" I asked, pulling my hand back.

"Nina, are you coming back to the kitchen?" the feisty woman asked.

"Maya, this is Ethan West, a friend of the family and possibly the next governor of New York," Nina informed her friend.

"I know who he is," Maya answered.

Chapter 4

Ethan

"Thank you for acknowledging me. I can't say I have the same pleasure, Maya."

"And you never will. I've tried to get an interview with you, and you blew me off. So, again, you can keep the nice guy act for someone else," Maya fussed, rolling her eyes.

"I don't remember you asking for an interview. Did you contact my office?" I responded, crossing my arms over my chest.

Gage and Nina stared between the two of us.

"Auntie Maya, can we go shopping?" Tailynn asked.

Maya placed a hand on her hip, glaring at me. "Not today, baby. I have too much work to catch up on." Maya headed back toward the kitchen, with Tailynn and Nina following her.

"I can tell already," Gage hinted, pointing at Maya leaving out of the room.

"Tell what?" I questioned.

"You two are going to butt heads every second like me

and Nina, then eventually you'll wear her down and get married."

"What!" I scoffed at his idiot statement.

"Reminds me of how Nina and I got started. We clashed a few times until she realized she was in love with me," Gage commented.

I motioned for him to shut up. I would never get married—and especially not to a woman like that. "She's not my type. Anyway, I need to leave for an appointment I forgot I set up."

Heading toward the door, he followed me, Thalia still in his arms. "Just wait and see."

I opened the door right as Maya was coming toward us to leave with her purse on her shoulder.

"Whoever you're going to meet, make sure you strap up. We don't need any little Ethans running around if you're running for governor," Gage joked.

Maya stopped in her tracks at the mention of running for governor. "Another billionaire running for governor of New York," Maya said, shocked, as we both stepped out the door and headed to our cars.

"If I am, then what do I have to do to get your vote, Maya?" I teasingly asked, holding the driver's door open for her, then leaning in and closing the space between us.

"Mr. West, you can't handle the list of complaints I have. If I recall from the latest press headlines, you're in and out of relationships. Your family is constantly in the media after destroying some neighborhood for their personal gain."

"Can't believe everything you read, Maya."

"And you can't believe I would fall for your little good guy role, Ethan. Can I go now?" she challenged, leaning into the doorframe.

Stepping back, I let her get in the car and shut the door. I placed my hands in my pockets, watching her drive off.

Thirty minutes, later I pulled up to the hotel and got out of the car, giving the valet my keys. Heading into the hotel, I went up to the penthouse and knocked on the door.

Madelyn opened the door, wearing her black thong and high heels, her small breasts staring back at me. I smirked, walking inside as she pulled me in and closed the door. She teased me, kissing me alongside my neck and trying to kiss my lips.

I pulled back, shaking my head. "Madelyn, you know I don't kiss."

"Ethan... please... we've been doing this dance for months. We should just make this exclusive—especially if you're planning on running for governor. It would look better to the public if you had a girlfriend on your arm," Madelyn pouted, sliding her hands into my pants and stroking my dick.

Madelyn is my go-to person I call when I'm in the mood for companionship. Did I date a lot? No. I called it getting what I need when I want it and not leading any of them on thinking I'd ever commit. The longest relationship I ever had was with Hannah Miller, a woman that tried to control me and turn me into something I wasn't. I wasn't impressed with her family's money and thinking I would become this dynasty and have our families joined together. She was obsessed with herself and making things all about her in our relationship. We dated for three years and in the end, I realized she was all about appearances.

"Focus on taking care of him, Madelyn. I don't have time for your pouting and shit. You know better than anyone I don't do the kissing thing, let alone dating." I pushed her down to the floor by her shoulder as she unbuckled my pants, taking my dick out.

She licked her lips and took me into her mouth. I closed my eyes, feeling her warm mouth as she sucked from the tip of my dick while fondling my balls.

"Mmmm..." she moaned as she placed her hand on her left breast, squeezing her nipple.

* * *

The next day, I was sitting in my office with Tim, going over an official letter announcing my intention of running for governor. Tim had set up a small focus group a few weeks earlier, asking what people look for in their local politicians. He asked what they thought of a single man with money running for governor. Rich men didn't fare well in the public eye if they put out a message of wanting to help, but then took money from large corporations and never did anything with it. So, I promised myself to use my own money and really help clean up our city.

I always wanted to help the community in some way after years of seeing politicians lie, steal, and claim to want to help, only to end up taking money from big corporations and not help anyone. Also, because I saw how my mother continued working and overseeing different charities. She had a true love of helping. Even though she came from money, that didn't stop her from giving back. She raised us to help whoever needed it.

I started by investing in local free clinics as a private

donor. No one knew, and I liked it that way. Then I started paying for lunches for kids that came from financially constrained homes.

"Once you make this announcement, you can't go back. I'll ask you one last time; Are you sure about this? Because the campaign trail is exhausting and long," Tim explained, passing over the formal paperwork.

Working over the details of the fucked-up loan that Richard got my business involved with, took a few calls and promises to do an overhaul of the loan process for the entire company. Eventually, Tim got the newspaper to retract the fake engagement story with a promise that I would give them an exclusive story on my campaign announcement.

"Do you have a moment, sir?" Carol, my assistant asked.

I needed someone I could trust to help get through the mess Richard left after I fired most of the staff managers he put in place.

"What do you have?"

"Nothing major, but Richard was stealing from the bank."

"Damn it!"

"I'm surprised no one said anything. His work was so shoddy."

"How much?"

"About a million and five."

"This wouldn't look good if word got out."

"Exactly, you've come too far."

"All right, I'll transfer the money back into the account, I want you to contact Genesis and see who he uses for auditing and then get Tim up to date about all of this before anything leaks out. Also, I need you to get my cousin up to date on things. If he's taking over, I want him ready to handle any questions that come out."

"You got it, sir."

Chapter 5

Maya

"**M**mmm... keep going," I whispered through a moan.

Douglas wasn't the best with his oral skills, but he had money and spoiled me. So, once he left, I'd take care of myself with the vibrator Nina told me to purchase from Nicole's sex shop.

"Who's your man, baby?" Douglas questioned again for the fifth time whenever we met up to have sex. He thinks he'll catch me slipping and agree to us being a couple.

I snapped back, "Douglas, focus, please." I pushed his head farther in, making sure he hit my spot—even though I doubted he would. I had already learned to fake an orgasm with him to get him done faster and out of my house.

He did spend five-thousand dollars on me today, though.

"Baby, come on. Take care of him for me," Douglas said, pointing toward the erection in his pants.

I climbed out of the bed pulling my panties up.

"Sorry, Dougie, I'm not feeling well. I'll take a rain check," I said, walking toward the bedroom door to lead him out. He groaned angrily, standing up to button his shirt back up.

"Maya, you're tripping. Last time we had sex was two months ago. I'm starting to think you only want me for my money," Douglas whined.

"Douglas, if that was true, I would have left you alone a long time ago, sweetie. Let me remind you that you're not my boyfriend. If I feel like having sex, I will, and right now, I don't. You know the way out," I answered, irritated that he was begging for sex—something he wasn't good at anyway.

"Fine, call me when you're free," Douglas muttered, leaving out of my room and down the stairs to the front door.

Walking to my closet, I picked up my bag, grabbed my computer and sat back on the bed. I got another email from my bosses at FBX about restructuring, and my show might get canceled unless the ratings improved. I was thinking of doing a week of interviews with other influencers like me, and I had plans to get more celebrity guests. Nina said she spoke with Gage about having some of his teammates come on the show—*if* I didn't do the ambush type of interview I did with him a year ago.

I agreed, but the biggest guest I wanted was Ethan West. Ever since I saw him at Nina's place last week, I had him on my mind. That asshole pissed me off, thinking he could get me into bed without putting in any effort with his little comment of what it would take for an interview. But he would be great for ratings. His public persona was a mystery, besides a few tabloid headlines linking him with gorgeous women. He never did interviews or went to clubs; as far as I knew, he didn't go out and party like the bachelor the tabloids portrayed him to be.

Clicking on an email, I saw an invitation from Scottie for the fundraiser they had coming up. I chuckled as I remembered the last time I went when Gage paid for a date with Nina. Messaging the group, I asked who was going, and where they were sitting.

Me: *Hey, are you all going to the fundraiser?*

Nicole: *Yep. Free alcohol, of course.*

Nina: *What happened to you fasting?*

Me: *That lasted for a day. Nicole, did Nina have you drinking that nasty green smoothie?*

Nicole: *Nina thinks she's the Martha Stewart of our group now because of the twins and eating healthy.*

Scottie: *Did she make you that vegan lasagna?*

Diya: *I thought it was good.*

Me: *LOL! That was not lasagna. It was cardboard spaghetti.*

Nicole: *Diya, stop lying to her. You know you fed that food to your dog.*

Nina: *What!*

Me: *Hello. Right now, we're talking about the fundraiser. Scottie, what single rich men did you invite?*

Nicole: *Sorry, Ni-Ni.*

Diya: *I confessed to you in private about that.*

Me: *I'm dead.*

Scottie: *OMG! Nicole, stop, girl. Ni-Ni, we appreciate this new lifestyle, but we didn't ask for it.*

Nina: *All right, I'm over all of you. I have lunch to make for my kids, thank you very much.*
Nicole: *Give my nieces and nephew a kiss for me.*
Me: *What about the list of eligible bachelors?*
Scottie: *Genesis didn't tell me who he invited. His assistant set it up.*
Me: *Scottie...*
Scottie: *Sorry, bestie.*
Me: *I guess you don't love me.*

I sent the last message and closed out of the conversation. Tossing the phone on the bed, I stood and headed to the bathroom to freshen up and get ready for work. Once we finished shooting, I needed to look for a dress for the charity event. I had to make sure I strutted in with all eyes on me, letting everyone know who Maya Armstrong was.

* * *

Two hours later, I placed my purse on my desk and grabbed the caramel frappe out of my assistant's hand. "Don't tell Nina I had this, she's on a health kick and torturing all of her friends."

"No problem, boss," Clarissa, my longtime assistant, replied. She was hired before I came on, and we hit it off thanks to our shared love of fashion. "Douglas is looking for you."

Douglas was the station manager and executive producer of my show. Yes, I had sex with someone I worked with, and I regretted it every day. He wore me down and promised not to get attached, but you saw how that ended up.

"What's the meeting about?"

"The lineup of your guests for the new season. He has some ideas about getting more musicians on the show."

"I bet he does," I murmured as I headed to the conference room with Clarissa behind me.

"Are you excited about the fundraiser? It's the talk of the town and all-over social media with people talking about who's going to be there," Clarissa asked, opening the door of the conference room. Douglas stopped talking as I came inside and took a seat on the opposite side of him.

"Nice of you to join us, Maya," Tonya said nastily, flipping her blonde hair to the side.

I liked to call Tonya "my work nemesis." She was becoming a pain in my ass because her show came on after mine, and she didn't have the same budget, so she thought I slept my way to the top—which was completely false because I didn't start seeing Douglas until after he was hired a year ago.

"You look lovely today, Tonya. I see your roots are sprouting. You may want to get your color refreshed," I replied sarcastically.

"Ladies, please save your bickering for another time. We have business to discuss. Maya, who do you have lined up for guests? I need a complete rundown for the next two weeks of what you have planned," Douglas demanded.

Clarissa pulled her notepad out passing me a sheet with potential guest names. "I'm still waiting on confirmation, but Sammy Sin, Jalessa, and Mira of the girl group Exposure might confirm. As you know, I have a few more guests and the upcoming fundraiser that may bring in a good amount of media attention."

"So, basically, the same guests you've had in the past," Tonya said snidely.

"Whether or not we like each other Tonya, you could probably take some lessons and get your ratings up, boo," I spat, pointing a finger in her face.

Douglas slammed his hand down on the table and we all jumped in nervousness. "Maya, she's right, those guests have been here about three or four times. We need something fresh. Anyone else on that list?" Douglas questioned, narrowing his eyes.

"She doesn't have anyone, Douglas. Let me have her time slot. I have guests for the next two months ready to confirm if you agree."

A scowl crossed my face and I wanted to jump up and smack her across the face for getting in my business.

"Ethan West!" I shouted, loudly. Everyone in the room looked over at me.

"Bullshit!" Tonya yelled harshly.

Douglas glared at her. "Are you talking about Ethan West of West Banking?" Douglas inquired.

I nodded in response.

"Uh... yeah, I mean, he hasn't agreed yet, but—"

Douglas put his hand up to stop me from talking. "So, you don't have him confirmed, and you're wasting my time."

"No, but he's friends with my friend, and we'll both be at the Maguire fundraising charity this week. The perfect time to get him alone and ask about a one-on-one interview."

"She's lying, Douglas; you can't believe her," Tonya snarled, folding her arms across her chest.

"Ethan West is running for governor of New York;

we'd be stupid not to get him on the show," Douglas explained.

"Seriously, Douglas?" Tonya spat.

"Tonya, you should take notes from me and learn how to get the big guests," I said, smirking and flipping my hair to the side. "I had Gage Young last year, and I can promise I'll get Ethan West. If you need help, I could give you some tips."

"Ladies, can we please act like adults here? Tonya, ignore Maya. And Maya, get that interview because if you don't, I can assure you that someone will be ready to step in and take over," Douglas exclaimed, standing to leave and grabbing his paperwork.

Tonya and I sat, staring at each other.

"Listen, at one point I was in your same situation."

"What situation is that, Maya?"

"Trying to be the star, getting your name in lights, winning the awards. I can go on and on. Tonya, you're not the only girl in this business trying to be on top."

"Is that what you think?"

I leaned over the conference table. "That's what I know."

"So, you worked your way up from your little blog and networking to be the host of a midday basic-cable station show without sleeping your way to the top?"

"Aww, I see the problem now."

"What problem?" Tonya glared at me as I walked around toward the door.

"You think I slept my way to get here and not the long nights, studying, researching and hounding executives and publicists."

"Say what you want, but Douglas should have fired you a long time ago."

"Maybe you should rethink spreading nasty rumors because I would hate to get you fired. One thing we can agree on is Douglas doesn't like having his business out in the open—especially from someone who works for him."

Tonya stood up heading toward me, getting in my face. "I dare you," I replied, opening the door and leaving her alone with a hard glare on her face.

I sauntered off to my office to finish up for the day. Once I turned my computer off and picked up my purse and keys, I left to go to my parents' house to meet Kasey. She left me a voice message earlier about dinner.

Twenty minutes later, I parked in front of my childhood home. The brick, one-story house still held up. It was the first home my father built for my mom after living in apartments throughout their early marriage. Kasey's pink Beetle was parked out front. Picking up my purse, I took the key out of the ignition and closed the door.

Heading into the house, I smelled the aroma of fresh-cut flowers. I had to give my mother props for keeping the house updated and nice with new furniture—except for my dad's favorite reclining chair that sat in the corner with his beer holder on the side.

"Maya, thank God you're here." Kasey came over to hug me.

"Where is she?"

"In the kitchen on the phone gossiping as usual."

"Where's Dad?"

"She sent him to the store to get some canned corn. I swear he needs to divorce her."

"What did she do now?" I asked, taking off my jacket, hanging it up on the coat rack.

"She's forcing me to go on a stupid date with one of

Dad's church members because he has money." Kasey plopped down on the couch next to me.

"Kasey, did you hear me?" my mother shouted, walking into the living room. "Maya, what are you doing here?" she asked, stepping in front of the TV, and facing us.

"I like what you did with the place. I see Dad's money is really paying off."

"Mind a child's place."

"I would if I was a child, Hazel."

"Maya!" Kasey warned me, nudging me in the arm.

"No, don't warn her."

"Mom, please," Kasey muttered.

"You will call me Mother."

The door opened and I jumped up, ignoring her words to run and hug my father.

"Hey, My-My," my father said.

"Hey, Pops."

"How long you been here?" he questioned, walking over to my mother and kissing her on the forehead, then Kasey, passing her the bag of groceries.

"Not long. Kasey wanted to talk before I head home, and I haven't seen you in a week, so this was the perfect time to see my favorite people."

A suggestion of annoyance hovered in my mother's eyes. "Michael, come to the kitchen please," Mother demanded, scowling at me.

Kasey passed me the bag of corn and tried to walk off.

"What?"

"I didn't ask you here to fight with her. I just need a way to get out of this date."

"Say no," I replied, sitting back down on the couch.

"I did, but you know how she is. Can't you go with me on this date? Maybe a group thing."

"Child, I'm twenty-nine years old. I don't do group dates. Besides, I'm not dating anyone right now, so getting a last-minute thing wouldn't work."

"You're no help."

"Maybe Scottie or Diya has someone they can hook you up with instead of the guy Mom's hooking you up with. I know Talbot has a cousin named Daiton."

"The tattoo guy, right? I saw Gage in an advertisement for his shop. I know Nina has no complaints with having him on her arm."

"Gage is Gage."

"What does that mean?" Kasey asked, shoving me in the side.

"It means all of my friends have some sexy men at home and I'm still not dabbling my toe around the field."

"So, Maya Armstrong is telling me no guy has caught your attention out of that circle?"

"I didn't say no one has my attention. I'm just not reacting to anything."

"Who?"

"Who?"

"Spill it and tell me what guy you are lusting over right now."

I groaned in a vague hint of disapproval in myself for even thinking him up. "Ethan West," I mumbled, lowly under my breath.

"My-My and Kasey, come eat dinner," my father said.

"Coming."

"The banker who's running for governor? He's cute."

"Whatever. And if you tell anyone, I will deny it," I whispered, jumping up and going into the kitchen to eat.

Chapter 6

Ethan

I was standing inside my office, looking out at everyone in the city going about their day, waiting for everyone to congregate in the conference room. I was formally announcing my intention to run for office, and I was hesitant because of how intrusive the media could get with my family and digging up my past dirt.

There was a knock at my door. I turned to look at Claire, my assistant, coming inside with Tim behind her.

"Mr. West, it's time," she stated, passing me the speech she stayed up late typing to get right after I redrafted it four times.

Tim reached his hand out to shake mine. "Remember, keep it simple, short, and honest."

"What is the media temperature right now?"

"Same as usual. They want to know if you're really running as an Independent, who you are sleeping with, and how your family feels about this."

"So same as any normal Monday," I said, reading over the notes. "Did you get in contact with Scottie Maguire?"

Tim stiffened at my question; I knew he didn't like me

bringing in another senior advisor for my campaign. But after seeing the early numbers from the first Gallop poll, I was in the bottom ten candidates whom people would be interested in voting for. After talking it over with Genesis, I decided to bring Scottie on, since she dealt with regular people and knew what they wanted, and they listened to her advice. I thought it would be good to do a few ask-and-answer sessions, and then eventually have her on the campaign trail, setting up town hall meetings with voters.

It was lost on me what people would think of some out of the blue rich guy thinking he could buy his way into winning. I was determined to earn every vote.

"I really don't think we need her. Maybe if we find ourselves really behind. At this moment, we need to test the waters and focus on the bigger donors," Tim answered.

"What do you think, Garret?"

His assistant, Garret, was fresh from coming off a local city council campaign for the Manhattan district. I asked Tim about bringing on someone younger that knew what the young voters would want. Garret loved the outdoors, nature, hiking, snowboarding, and numbers.

"Sir, to keep it real with you, the future is Generation Y. You need the young voters—specifically the undecided voters. We already know that since you're running as Independent, you'll get a small number of Conservative voters based on your family's name, and you're a rich, handsome, single guy, so the Liberal young women will for sure fall at your feet. The group you'll need to work to get on your side are the undecided voters in rural towns." He sat three documents on my desk. "I agree with you about Scottie. She has the ear of Genesis Maguire, and the friendship of the TV host, Maya Armstrong."

"Who is Maya Armstrong?"

Garret cleared his throat and pointed toward my television, asking permission to change the channel. I waved my hand for him to continue.

He stood up walking over to the television and changing it to FBX.

Welcome to Spotlight with Maya, I'm your host Maya Armstrong. I like to keep things real, raw, and honest with you. Sit back, relax, and let's get started.

She was sitting at a desk with her hair pulled slightly to the left in a side ponytail. High cheekbones, perfectly shaped white teeth with her pouty red lips ready to be devoured. You could get lost in her eyes with how they needed someone to tame that pretty mouth. I needed to shake off this feeling. The last thing I needed was to be attracted to a loud mouth, overbearing woman that thought she knew everything.

Okay ladies, we have to stop letting men get the goodies without committing. How many times have you found yourself checking your man's phone? Don't lie now. That's why I refuse to let anyone walk all over me.

Then she opened her mouth.

"Turn it off," I demanded.

"Isn't she the gossip blogger?" Tim queried.

"She does different guest interviews and celebrity gossip. She had Gage Young on the show about a year ago," Garret exclaimed.

"Wasn't that a gotcha moment exposing his family's business?"

Garret thought about it and nodded in answer. "It was, but that's what makes this so perfect. If you have them on your team early to combat the media invasion you'll receive, you can't lose because they'll already have all of your secrets laid out before the major news outlets can do anything."

"I don't have any secrets."

Garret and Tim both looked at me in jest. "What?"

But I'm lost in thought, totally zoned out, sitting at the edge of my desk. Listening intently to her sharp, sassy, strong-willed voice. Thinking of her on her knees with my dick in her mouth, and hands tied behind her back with nothing on but my red tie. "Everyone has secrets, Ethan. It's all a matter of how you go about controlling the narrative," Tim implied, standing to turn the TV up and listening to Maya.

"Huh," I said.

I held my hand up for him to stop talking.

Voting is the one thing you can control that will have an effect over your entire life. I pledge to keep you all informed and if you follow me on this journey, we'll take you behind the scenes at some of these campaigns for the good and bad of politics. I'm here to let you know that this season on Spotlight, we will delve into so much more beyond what you've seen so far. Our show has exclusive content streaming on all social media pages and my blog is back up for the new season. So, get ready because Maya will keep it real, raw, and unfiltered. - Maya Armstrong.

"We'll discuss this Maya later. I need to talk with my team first, and see if Scottie would be interested, I already received the invitation to the charity event this year."

"Are you making a donation this year?" Tim wondered, falling in step with me as we prepared to leave my office.

I passed my assistant's desk. "Can you contact Scottie Maguire for me and see if she'll do lunch next week? I need to put some things into place before I commit to bringing on more help for the campaign."

This was my main building that I ran all my branches from, plus my investments and real estate firms. I visited all my banks once a month to make sure things were running smoothly, but overall, everything happened at this main building. I had it built by an old friend, Isaiah Reed. He was a local architect and was married to Vanessa Andrews, a fashion designer and stylist to the stars. They had a baby a year ago, as well.

Most of my friends were having kids and getting married. It was crazy to think of Gage Young, the playboy from college, now married with twins—and to someone as gorgeous as Nina. I chuckled to myself. I could still recall his facial expression when I said I went out on a blind date with Nina. He was ready to kick my ass. Even though we didn't have any sexual chemistry, Nina and I had stayed friends, and I had met her family. Gage, of course, was annoyed, but eventually he got over it after he saw I wasn't a threat to his marriage. Since then, we truly had become friends.

I wonder if they'll be at the fundraiser, I thought.

"I am," I answered, remembering Tim's question.

"Did you take care of that Hannah situation?" Tim pointed out.

"I talked with her to get it retracted and fired Richard."

"So why am I looking at her on *Access Entertainment* talking about you two discussing the campaign?"

"What are you talking about?"

"She's determined," Garret stated.

"Doesn't she have a job? What did you do to her?" Tim insisted, turning the clip off on his phone.

"She cheated on me two years ago and wants me to take her back. I won't so she's causing problems to get my attention. Ignore her."

"We need this nipped in the bud fast. "

"I agree, but right now I need you to make sure my announcement is set up and let me get in here to tell my employees that I'm finally ready to step down."

Shaking off the thought, I opened the door of my clear glass conference room. Inside sat all my top executives, and the managers of each branch. I walked to the middle of the conference room table as all eyes were on me.

I knew the news had spread throughout the office and some of my bank branches that I was thinking of running for office, and everyone was wondering whether I would sell my businesses or not. I was very transparent—and some people even said bossy, and stubborn—when it came to my business. But I earned that right because I built this business into what it was today.

I still hadn't told my family officially because I needed time to prepare myself mentally and to decide whether this was going to be something that I could see going far or just as a one-time thing. But after the many conversations I had with local employees and seeing how they were still struggling—even with the paycheck and health insurance I gave out—I knew I had to do something to make this city better.

I cleared my throat, and the entire room went silent.

"I want to thank you all for coming on such short notice, I know you're all busy and I appreciate you dropping everything to meet with me. I won't hold you up for too long, so as you've all probably heard throughout the building because we all know Gladys in accounting gossips like a high school teenager..."

Everyone laughed and nodded at my true statement. She was one of the oldest employees there, and she reminded me of Doretha, Nina's grandmother.

"I have decided to run for governor of New York."

The entire room was in shock based on the wide eyes, furrowed brows, and mouths gaped open.

"This was a decision I didn't make lightly. I knew the media would try to hammer you all with questions about me and my personal life. So, before that happens, I wanted to let you know that I prefer to keep my personal life out of this. My business will continue to run. My brother, the Vice President, will take over. If I win the election, then he will officially be appointed the CEO of West Banks and Investments."

Cody Sprout from the West Coast branches raised his hand to speak. I waved for him to continue. "Your brother has only been in the role for a year or two. Wouldn't it be better if you have someone who has years of experience running things while you're gone?"

"Cody, no one likes you, the amount of years doesn't matter. I have years of experience from working under my brother at his real estate business and his banks as a manager. The last thing you need to worry about is me," Jared, my brother spat.

I trudged back into my office.

"Sir, this was left for you." Carol passed me a yellow envelope as I walked inside of my office with my campaign team behind me.

My steps slowed as I opened the envelope, and pulled

out a newspaper with a report showing Hannah and I on the front page with nude photos of us.

"Tim, get Hannah in my office now," I shouted, slamming the newspaper down on the desk.

"Hannah your ex?" he muttered, stepping forward picking up the newspaper. "When did this happen? I just spoke with you yesterday."

"It's not true. She's obviously lost her mind and is trying anything she can to get my attention. I want her in my office, and I want those pictures deleted from everywhere."

"Doesn't seem like a bad idea," Garret exclaimed, taking the paper out of Tim's hands.

I ran a hand down my face. "Garret, if you want to stay on the campaign, I suggest you don't bring that up again."

Chapter 7

Maya

It was a windy but bright and sunny day. There was a small crowd of protestors standing in the back of the building with signs reading, "Pretty Boy" and "No More Billionaires." I figured this wasn't the warm welcome he was looking for, so I pushed through, trying to keep my earpiece in my ear, and Larry my camera guy, close by.

No more billionaires!

No more pretty boys!

I felt a tap on my shoulder. "Maya, make sure you stay close, this crowd could get vicious."

As the screaming and shouting continued, I took a few photos on my phone as I saw Ethan standing at the podium, waving at his supporters. He looked sexy in his dark blue Brooks Brothers suit. I bit down hard on my bottom lip to control the nasty thoughts in my head. Larry tapped me on the shoulder.

"Aren't you Maya Armstrong?" asked a young woman in jeans and a red shirt that read: "Ethan West for Governor 2020."

"I am."

"Can I get a picture please?"

She quizzed. "Sure, if you can tell me why you're voting for Ethan West."

"He's cute!" She grinned.

I hiked a brow. "And?"

"What else is there?" She threw her hands up.

"How old are you?" I asked.

"Twenty."

"Well, I suggest you research your candidates. What's your name?'

"Anna."

"Okay, Anna, you seem smart, so let me give you some advice. If you pick your candidates for office the same way you pick your hair color or dates, then you'll have a very lonely life. Because this color is dual and not inspiring the same as the candidates running for office in New York."

"What about the porn, Governor?" a protestor yelled out.

Larry scrambled to get the camera plugged up to capture his reaction.

"Ladies and gentlemen, thank you for coming today," Ethan said.

"He's so dreamy!"

"I'm formally announcing my intention to run for governor of New York," Ethan stated.

"Oh...yeah!" the crowd screamed.

"Larry, you get that." I pointed to the left side of the crowd jumping up and down.

"My goal is to fund this campaign on my own without corporate lobbyists. This campaign is bought by the people and for the people," Ethan said.

"What about your nude photos?" a protestor shouted.

"Mr. West won't be answering any questions today. Those photos are fake," his campaign manager explained into the mic.

"Boo!"

"Make sure you're getting this, Larry!" I yelled over the noise.

"Let me say, before I go any further, I made my money the honest way by working hard. I don't owe anybody anything. I'm no longer with that woman in the photos. At one time, we did take those pictures as a consensual couple. She released them as payback for not reconciling. I don't work too well with being black-mailed. Now, I'm more interested in figuring out how we can cut taxes for the middle class and put our kids back in school, lower housing costs, and clean up the homeless problem. Now, we can sit here all day and talk about some nude photos, or we can come up with some solutions, and you can vote for me as your next governor to take us into the future together," Ethan informed the crowd.

The entire crowd clapped and screamed in excitement. He waved.

"He's good. The crowd loves him," Larry expressed.

"He's okay," I replied.

"We should try and get in the back to do a quick interview. Follow me."

We pushed through the crowd heading to the side of the stage as Ethan and his team came down the stairs.

"Ethan West! Ethan!" I screamed, trying to get through the security detail.

"It's all right. I can talk to her."

Larry started rolling his camera. "Mr. West, how are

you feeling about the crowd?" I asked, putting the mic up to him to answer.

"Maya, you can call me Ethan."

"I prefer Mr. West... sir."

"Sir. Huh."

"Can you answer my question?"

"Off the record."

"Ethan, we need to go," his campaign manager said.

"Tim, this is Maya Armstrong, the host of *Spotlight with Maya* that Garret was talking about," Ethan explained.

"That's nice, but we need to get things set up at the office."

"Are you going to the fundraiser?" Ethan asked me.

"What?" I was surprised by his question. I waved for Larry to turn the camera off.

"I said, will I see you at the charity auction Genesis and Scottie are throwing?"

"I'm going, yes. Now can you answer my question?"

"What would you like to know, Maya?"

"I would like to know if the photos were sent on purpose to get attention for your campaign."

He chortled at my question.

He moved in, closing the gap between us.

"Do you think I need to put nude photos of myself out to get attention, Maya?"

"I don't know what you would do for someone's attention."

"Someone or you?"

"Mr. West," I whispered slowly, searching around, making sure no one was watching us.

"Ethan."

"Mr. West, I would like to get a one-on-one interview

with you. My audience and yours would love to see the two of us sitting together to answer the major questions."

"What do I get out of it?" His gaze was riveted on my face, then moved over my body.

"What do you want?"

"Ethan, I hate to interrupt you and Miss Armstrong, but we really need to go!" Tim exclaimed.

Clearing his throat, he stuck his hand out for me to take. "Call my office and have Tim schedule you some time. Also, tell Scottie thanks again for meeting with me."

"Scottie..."

I watched as security escorted him to his limo to leave.

"You ready to go?" Larry asked.

"Yeah."

Larry looked over his shoulder. "I like him."

"Larry, you like anything."

He shrugged at my comment, not disagreeing as we strolled to the crew van to go back to the studio.

In my efforts to make sure my show's ratings ticked back up, I stayed a little longer with the editor and Larry to go through the footage from the day's rally. "How was the crowd today?"

"He's good for the camera," Larry answered.

I sat in the editing booth with Larry and Nigel. Nigel started at the station about ten years ago, when it was mostly news and cooking shows. Once the station branched out to get the younger audience, Nigel had to adapt, and sometimes it wasn't the best because he liked to stick to simple cuts and nothing over-the-top. Unlike me.

"I think he's smart, charismatic."

Nigel fast forwarded to the end section of the protestors. "Rich," Nigel said.

"What do we know about his family?"

Larry passed me a piece of bubble gum.

"He comes from a wealthy background, but mostly made his money by investing and starting his banking business.

"Is he really engaged?" Nigel queried.

"He looks like the type who has a Stepford wife at home with two-point-five kids," Larry joked.

"The uptight, 'probably only sticks to missionary' type." I chortled, standing up grabbing my purse, and looking for my keys. It was getting late and I hadn't eaten anything since earlier that morning.

"I'm going out for food. You guys want anything from Comet's?"

"Roast beef sandwich and Coke," Larry said as I walked out.

"Make that two!" Nigel shouted.

Comet's was normally quiet around eight at night, but right now, it was bustling with a large crowd. Photographers were outside, taking pictures and blocking the walkway.

Opening the door, I greeted the hostess to let her know I called in my order for pickup already. She motioned for me to head to the front counter. Looking around the room, I noticed some familiar faces from the corner of my eye.

Waving, I walked over to greet my favorite couple.

"Well, now I see why the paparazzi are outside."

Scottie leaned up to return my hug. I walked over and greeted Genesis with a hug.

"I wish they'd find some real news to look into, instead of following us around all the time," Scottie said.

Seeing three plates of food, I pointed at the steak and potatoes inquiring who they were having dinner with.

"Who else is with you guys?"

"Sorry about that. Tim needed me to sign off on some interviews," Ethan said, coming up behind me.

I swallowed the lump in my throat, before turning around and taking in his casual attire. His black shirt was open with no tie, nice jacket, black slacks, and minimal jewelry. He was six two, lean muscled, athletically built, broad shoulders. He stood with a sexy smirk on his face, hands in his pockets.

"Maya, we keep meeting. I'm starting to think you're stalking me."

Rolling my eyes at his comment, I turned back to Scottie and Genesis ignoring Ethan.

"How long have you two been here?"

"Not very long, our food just came out," Scottie replied.

"Genesis, I have my dress for the charity auction. But what type of auction are we talking about? Are you doing the bachelor-and-bachelorette auction like last year with Nina and Gage?"

"No, this year, we're doing a silent auction, and then performances from some musicians. I decided I didn't want my wife and her friends running around, bidding on single men."

"Any single friends coming?" I asked, ignoring Ethan's longing stare.

"Do you need a date, Maya?" Ethan questioned, taking a seat. The waitress came over and handed me the bag of food.

"Here's your order, ma'am," the waitress said, and I handed her a tip.

"Thank you. Mr. West, you're not my type."

"What type is that?"

"The cocky, 'I-am-man-and-you're-my-woman' type. Wanting a wife to stay at home and give him a house full of kids, and she can't work, because she needs to have his food ready on time so that you both can eat and talk about his day, then get the kids to bed and do it all over again. *That* type."

The look on his face almost made me burst out laughing.

"She's good," Scottie said and we high-fived.

"Reminds me of somebody I know," Genesis responded, and Scottie nudged him in the arm.

He licked his lips, standing back up. "Let me walk you out."

"I can walk myself out, Mr. West."

"I'd like to speak with you about a private matter, and, seeing as how you owe me, I think a walk is a part of repaying your debt," Ethan countered.

"*Owe* you? Excuse me?" I spat.

"You two make a cute couple, try not to kill each other," Scottie said.

I furrowed my brows at Scottie. I could imagine this being a setup, but I knew Genesis wouldn't go along with one of Scottie's schemes.

"How do you figure I owe you?" Folding my arms over my chest, I leaned my weight on the other foot.

"You don't. I just liked to see that little twitch in your eye when you get upset, and how your cheeks puff out, and the sexy way you bite on your bottom lip." Ethan held the door open for me, following me out of the restaurant.

"The second we walk out together the photographers will have us married with kids by tomorrow morning," I remarked.

"Sounds like a good story to me."

"I want a sit-down interview," I demanded.

"I want a date," Ethan replied with a counteroffer, opening my car door.

"I don't date."

"Make an exception."

I leaned against the door, and he moved in close. The only thing separating us was the bag of food. The smell of his cologne was intoxicating. A part of me wanted to throw the rules out the window. But he was too high profile to be added to my list of playthings.

"I fuck." A chill ran up my spine.

"Obviously he's not doing it right, because the spark in your eye at me asking for a date intrigued you."

"Do all the women fall at your feet, Mr. West?"

He leaned in closer, bending down to whisper in my ear. "You look sexy when you're pouting." He groaned, pushing a loose string of hair behind my ear.

Before I could respond, my stomach growled loudly, stopping me. "I need to get back to work."

"Look forward to seeing you at the auction. Save a dance for me," Ethan said, watching me get inside the car, place the key in the ignition, and drive off back to the studio. I intended to end my lonely night with two men who liked to talk about their old dating escapades during the 70's and 80's.

Chapter 8

Maya

After the last meeting with Douglas, I needed to grab interviews with some major guests to help keep my ratings up, so I didn't lose my spot to that bitch. But once we finished the segment on Ethan's campaign last night, I took the day off.

I'd recently redesigned my bathroom to include a large, sunken marble jacuzzi with my initials etched all around the room, plus two large mirrors, cabinets, and drawers for my hair and makeup products. Chante Moore played quietly in the background as I sat in the tub with cucumbers on my eyes, wearing a fresh facial mask. Candles were lit all around. My hair was wrapped in a scarf to keep from getting wet.

Taking a sip of my Moscato, I let the cool, sweet taste drain down my throat. "Mmmm, hits the spot."

Suddenly, Nina, Emery, and Scottie burst into the bathroom. "Maya!" they shouted. I became close with Emery and the Pierce family through Gage and Nina.

"Ahhhh!" I screamed, popping out of the tub, trying to cover up by pulling my knees to my chest.

"Get out of my bathroom!"

"Maya, we both change shitty diapers, the last thing you need to worry about is covering up. We've seen it all honey," Emery joked, taking a seat on the toilet and grabbing a piece of the strawberry.

With a furrowed brow I stared at her. "Really, Emery?"

Nina walked over and grabbed the Moscato glass and took a sip.

"I needed this," Nina said, sighing and patting her chest, bending down to grab a grape and some cheese.

"Uh-uh! You two leave and wait for me outside. I was having a perfectly good bath until you two decided to spoil my afternoon."

Emery stood up and walked closer to the tub with a sneaky grin on her face. I followed her eyes, and she went to grab for my little friend that I'd just bought a week ago and was getting ready to use today. We both went to reach for it, and she grabbed it first. Twisting around in excitement, she passed it to Nina.

"Ugh, I can't stand you two." I stood, grabbing a towel off the rack, and followed them out of the bathroom.

"I see we interrupted Maya time," Nina snickered and sat on the edge of my bed.

I ripped my nightgown off the back of the door and pulled my scarf off, shaking my hair out and grabbing my brush. I stepped in front of the mirror. "Ha-ha. What do you two heathens want?"

"Don't be like that, boo. I just left the softball game with Nina and the kids. Then we decided to see what Diya was up to at the shop. Your name came up, and we said, 'Let's go bug her before she gets the day going'."

Once my hair was wrapped in a high ponytail, I

grabbed a towel, dried off, and changed into a nude bra-and-panty set. I picked up the jeans and crop top I left on my bed, got dressed, and sat at my vanity mirror.

"What are Talbot and Diya up to? I've been meaning to go get my tattoo done one day this week," I reminded myself.

"Working as usual. I made sure they were still coming to the fundraiser. Marcus and Gage were there so we all had a little reunion. You know I think Marcus would make a cute date for you."

I grunted at her statement. I wiped away the excess face cream. I was going with light makeup today, since I was off. Even though I was in the public eye, I made sure I stayed looking presentable. I was a brand at the end of the day. Lightly dusting on Bobbi Brown foundation, I picked up my black eyeliner to make cat-eyes.

"What's wrong with Marcus?" Nina asked, standing up before coming toward me and reaching for the maroon eye palette. I slapped her hand away and she still took it out of my grip.

"No, you can't have it."

She didn't care and took it anyway. That's the problem; she knew I couldn't really argue because I was always taking one of her outfits or makeups.

"Where's Nicole?"

"She has a DJ job in Atlanta. I told her to take a friend with her to be on the safe side."

Nina's phone rang and she answered it on FaceTime. "Hey, babe."

"Where are you?" Gage asked, loudly, with the kids screaming in the background.

We all cackled at him, trying to watch all three kids. I knew they were probably tearing up Talbot's shop.

"I'm at Maya's hanging out."

"Come get your wife, Gage, and her friend too!" I pouted my lips, checking to make sure I didn't get any red lipstick on my teeth. Standing up, I walked to my shoe closet to get a pair of Christian Louboutin heels.

"Where are you going all dressed up, future wifey?"

I stood up hearing that voice and turned around flipping him off.

"Marcus, shut up."

"Maya, you know you love me, girl." Marcus chuckled, blowing me a kiss.

"If you were the last man on Earth, I wouldn't sleep with you."

"Marcus, do you have a date for the fundraiser this year?" Emery asked.

Shaking my head at the both of them, I waved them off before grabbing my purse and keys, ready to get my day started. Heading to the door, I leaned against it, waiting for them to follow.

"Oh Maya, you need a date, baby? I can add you to my roster."

Nina held the phone up toward me with Marcus grinning wide and showing all of his perfectly white teeth. I hung up the phone on him and turned to walk off. Don't get me wrong, Marcus was sexy as hell, but a damn manwhore and I didn't have time for that.

Nina's phone rang again as we walked down the stairs.

Heading out of my place, locking the door behind Nina, I hit the key fob so they could get inside the car then I walked around to the driver's side and put the key in the ignition, backing up and driving off.

"If that's Marcus again, tell him to first go check on

those child support cases he has pending before he steps to me."

"I'm not Marcus, but I'll be sure to ask him the next time I see him."

I froze at the deep, raspy voice. "Cat got your tongue, Maya?" Ethan taunted.

Stopping at the red light, I took the phone out of Nina's hand. "Ethan, did you decide on doing an interview for my talk show?" I tried to steer the conversation to a topic that wouldn't have my juices flowing in the grandma panties I was wearing.

"Did you decide to come with me as my date for the auction?" he countered, grinning, winking at me. It looked as though he was at his campaign office.

"One date, and I get an exclusive one-on-one interview, plus a tour of your campaign office," I demanded.

"Deal."

"Just like that?"

"Just like that," Ethan repeated.

"I don't trust how easy it was for you to give into my request."

"Maya, by the time our date is over, you'll more than trust me. I'll have you calling me—"

Before he could finish his statement, I muted the phone.

"Emery I think Maya wants to be alone," Nina teased, poking me in the arm.

"I think you're right, but first we need to go shopping. Tell your boyfriend I'll see him soon and it's our time now to hangout."

Flipping them both off, I unmuted the phone to tell Ethan goodbye.

"Bab..."

"Ethan! I'm not alone in my car and this conversation is not happening. I have to go."

"Where are you going?"

"Shopping."

"I advise you to get something not too revealing."

"I could have sworn my father's name was Michael Armstrong," I informed him, turning into the parking lot of Standfield Mall.

Pulling in close to the door, I turned the car off, unbuckled and got out as Ethan continued rambling on.

"I'm not, but I know the second I see you in a dress, I can't promise my hands, and lips won't be all over you. Even if another guy thinks of asking you out, then we'll have a bigger problem."

Deep down inside, I liked his little jealous streak. I was the type of woman that demanded all my guy's attention.

"Good thing I'm not your woman, right?" I insisted and hung up the phone, laughing with Scottie.

Nina shook her head in disappointment.

"What, Nina?"

"Ethan's going to get in that ass. Keep putting up this façade if you want to."

"I'm not putting up a façade. If he wants me then he'll have to do the chasing. I'm Maya Armstrong and she is well worth the fight."

"Okay, Maya. The minute you start talking in third person, you lose any credibility with me!" Emery exclaimed, striding through the automatic doors. Nina and I followed, seeing a display of dresses.

"What type of dress do you have in mind?" Nina questioned, picking through the evening gowns that Saks Fifth Avenue displayed.

"Something that shows off all my assets—the Ts *and* the A."

Catching my eye was a long, low-cut, black V-neck dress with off-the-shoulder sleeves. It captured my style in every way.

"This is it."

Nina and Scottie nodded holding it up under my neck to get a picture of what the entire ensemble would look like.

"Black high-heeled shoes or maybe something silver that stands out, with long, thin silver earrings, and your hair up in curls," Nina suggested.

"That would be perfect, Maya. Maybe we can find out what Ethan is wearing, and you guys could match. Like a prom date," Emery joked.

"Emery."

"Just a thought."

"Did you match with Jackson at your first time attending his event?" I asked.

Taking the dress out of Nina's hands, I continued looking around for backup dresses before we left and I dropped them both at home.

"I didn't. Jackson didn't mind. He understands I like to stand out in the crowd," Emery replied.

Observing the red, gold, and silver heels, I grabbed them all and decided to play around with multiple takes to see what worked best after getting my hair done.

* * *

Getting to my place after dropping the girls off, I took the clothes to my bedroom and called my sister to see how her date went.

"Hello."

"Hey, Maya."

"Where are you?" I questioned hearing loud noises in the background.

"Leaving out of the grocery store. Work was long and dealing with your mother constantly calling me about her little fix-me-up date, I needed a drink and food," Kasey explained.

"That's why I'm calling. Did the date go well?" I hung my dress up on the back of the closet door, then pulled each shoe out of the box and sat them next to the jewelry I was planning on wearing.

"I did, and it was a mess."

"Did he try anything with you? You know I can call the girls and we'll go out looking for him," I interrogated, sitting on the edge of the bed taking my shoes off.

"The man is so self-involved; he blows my mind. All we did was talk about him, and what his expectations are for when we get married."

"What!" I stood up fast about to grab my keys to go yell at my mother.

"Girl, your mother is ridiculous and controlling, honey. I politely told him no thank you, and to lose my number."

"Better you than me, because he would have left with a busted lip. Hazel Armstrong has lost her mind."

"I agree, but she's our mother."

"Your mother, I still think I'm adopted."

Kasey giggled at my comment.

"Anyway, I'm going to let you go, so you can get home safe, and I'll talk to you later, baby sister."

"All right, be good."

"I can never promise that. Bye, girl."

Chapter 9

———

Maya

Nina was grinning like something was funny. I couldn't stand my friend. This was a sign to put an ad in the paper to find new friends. I mean, they had apps for dating; something had to be created to find best friends, because these two were up to no good.

We'd all decided to have a little get-together at Nina's place, and Gage invited some of his friends over. Nina invited the one person I was avoiding.

"This is a set-up," I whispered in Diya's ear, pointing at all the sexy men, sitting outside and in the living room.

"Good thing you're spoken for, or this would be really weird," Diya yawned, wrapping her arms around Talbot as he approached with Ethan, holding a beer.

"How are you, Ethan?" Nina questioned.

Evaluating the area, I avoided all eye contact with him. My efforts didn't matter because he came and stood right in front of me anyway, cutting the distance between us.

"I'm good, Nina. How are you? How are the kids?" he asked her then peered into my eyes.

I cleared my throat.

"Something caught in your throat, Maya?"

"I'm fine, Mr. West," I answered matter-of-factly.

Scottie and Nina tried to suppress a laugh.

"Yes, you are."

Marcus, Gage, and Genesis walked over joining us.

"There's my future wifey," Marcus playfully gloated, standing next to me.

"Marcus, I think you are mistaken. Maya's spoken for already," Ethan snapped, jumping into Marcus's face.

Talbot, Gage, and Genesis shoved him away from Marcus.

"Wow, man, I'm just playing. Maya's my friend, we always kid around," Marcus stated.

"Ethan, cool off. He's just messing with Maya," Gage said, leaning down to kiss Nina on the cheek.

"Maya can talk for herself and she's single," I challenged, walking off into the kitchen, leaving everyone.

Opening the fridge, I grabbed a bottle of water and took a sip. Closing the fridge door, I jumped back, startled by Ethan, standing with a harsh glare on his face. I wanted to lick that pout off his cute face, but I was playing hard-to-get. His t-shirt hugged his muscular build, and his Nike jogging pants showcased the long, thick, tasty treat I knew he was hiding.

"Where do you get off telling people I'm spoken for?" I demanded. Stepping into his face, I pointed at his chest and he grasped my hand, kissing the back of my palm, making my anger flush away.

"You're cute when you're fussing at me."

"I'm cute when I'm mad or happy."

"You think very highly of yourself, I see."

"Yep."

"I like you, Maya."

I sauntered over to the living room after the rest of the guys went outside, and I took a seat on the couch.

"What are you afraid of?" Ethan inquired as he followed me.

"Nothing."

Turning the TV on, a reporter was running a story on Ethan and the photo scandal.

"Is that still going on?" I grilled.

He sighed, taking a seat next to me. "Unfortunately, it is. And my ex, Hannah, is driving me crazy. She's the one responsible for it, thinking I would take her back after denying everything. She was the one who cheated on me, and I wasn't sticking around to be with someone selfish and narcissistic."

"What if I told you I'm selfish and narcissistic, even a little bit crazy, like bust the windows in your car?"

He grinned at my question, stretching his arm behind the couch.

"I like crazy, not unpredictable. Hannah is unpredictable and vindictive."

"The campaign is looking good for you."

"It's still early and I'm feeling things out. Can I count on your vote?"

He picked the remote up and turned the TV off.

"It depends."

Leaning in close, he asked, "On what?"

"How our date goes, of course."

"Tell me about your family?"

"I'm the daughter of Michael and Hazel Armstrong.

You can say a daddy's girl and a mother's worst nightmare," I chuckled at my own joke.

"I have the same problems, except both my parents drive me up the wall. How old are you?"

"Is this a date? Because you're asking me all these personal questions, and you haven't even done an interview on my show." Standing up, I pulled my shorts down to stop them from riding up my thighs, and I noticed Ethan licking his lips.

"Never going to happen," I flirted, sashaying out making sure my ass was poked out just right.

"Never say never!" Ethan shouted.

I opened the door to my parents' home after leaving Nina and Gage's place. My father was in his recliner, watching the latest NBA game on the TV, and my mother was sitting on the couch opposite him, typing into her iPad.

After kissing my father on the cheek, I plopped down and hesitantly spoke to my mother. "Hello, Mother."

"Hey."

"Hazel." My father grunted at her response.

"What?"

"It's fine, Daddy."

"No, it's not, and I want you two to stop this now. I've forgiven and let the past go; it's time for you two to get out your feelings and be a mother and daughter again. You're too old for this back-and-forth arguing and carrying on. You'll send an old man to the grave early," my daddy argued, taking a sip of his beer.

"She's the one filling Kasey's head with nonsense, wanting her to be single and miserable like her. Do you know Percy called and told me Kasey blocked him from her phone? I can barely show my face in church," my mother retorted.

"That's because you'll catch on fire, you devil," I mumbled under my breath.

"Excuse me, little girl. What did you say?" Mother asked.

"Nothing."

Deep down, I knew I should try to rebuild my relationship with my mother, but the woman was crazy and thought the world revolved around her. Nina told me all the time to let the past hurt go but finding out your mother isn't the perfect human being you thought she was, opens your eyes.

"I like what he's trying to do for the city," my father interrupted my thoughts.

On the screen, a campaign slogan endorsed by Ethan played.

"I'm covering him for my show. Trying to get an interview for a sit-down one-on-one. Did you know he's friends with Gage and Nina?" I explained.

"That's nice, baby."

"How long are you going to cover makeup and fashion on TV? Why don't you get a real job doing something meaningful, like teaching or working at the church?" my mother asked.

"I'm on TV every day, giving my thoughts and opinions. It's more than playing dress-up, Mother."

"Hazel, leave her alone. She's happy. That's all that matters."

"This is one of the reasons why I hate coming over here and dealing with your judgmental tone. You've done nothing in life but cheat on Daddy and spend his money, and you still think what I do is so beneath meaningful work?" I screamed snidely.

She smacked me across the face.

"Hazel!" Father jumped out of his seat to get between us.

"No, it's fine, Daddy."

"Do you see how she talks to me, Michael?" my mother questioned, giving me a penetrating glare.

Hugging my father, I kissed him on the cheek, and he kissed me back on the forehead, shaking his head at the outcome of my visit. I hurried out of the house, heading home to drink a bottle of wine and find something—or *somebody*—to relieve my stress.

Chapter 10

Ethan

Hanging up with my attorney, I sighed in frustration. Hannah was continuing to get a response from the photographers and the media because of her family's name. It didn't help that my mother was making comments that she thought I needed to forgive Hannah and try to see things from her point of view. She said she had made mistakes herself when she was younger.

"Sir, are you ready?" Garret asked.

"Yeah. Is the limo ready?"

"Yes, and I took the liberty of setting up a few notes for when you walk the red carpet tonight."

"Thanks, how are the polling numbers looking?"

"The numbers are going up. Even with the scandal Hannah is trying to drum up, the women love you and the guys want to hang out and have a beer with you. The problem is the older crowd in the rustbelt. You're looked at as young without years in politics behind you," Tim answered honestly.

Genesis graciously let me bring my team along, in case the media hounded me.

"Hopefully with Scottie coming on board and a few sit-down interviews, we can sway some voters my way."

"I think with Genesis endorsing you tonight and local business owners like Talbot and Gage's celebrity status, people will really start to get in line and support you. We knew as a fresh face, the sharks would be out. Only problem we didn't see was your ex-girlfriend, Hannah, chomping at the bit."

"How did you know Genesis was endorsing me? We'd just talked about it briefly at Gage's get together the other day," I inquired.

"His assistant called me and explained that he would be making an official announcement at the event tonight seeing as all of the media and important people in the financial industry would be there."

"I'm still not taking funds from corporate people or lobbyists, Tim," I informed.

He motioned that he understood. "I know, but a picture of you standing next to Gage and Genesis on stage can make big numbers for us going into the next campaign event. The other candidates are still scrambling to make a name for themselves, so you have an advantage there. But at the same time, it can hurt you to be a single billionaire with no plans to marry and running for office with a radical agenda."

"What's radical about paying for education and making sure medical care is afforded to all?"

"Nothing wrong with it, Ethan. But you're an Independent. That scares the old base of both political powers. You have no ties to either side, so they feel you're not beholden to anyone, which makes you unpredictable.

They can't guess how you'll run the state," Tim reminded me.

"He has a point, sir," Garret said, holding the door open as I walked out of the campaign office to our waiting limo.

* * *

At the Maguire Charity Fundraiser, a reporter announced to the camera, "Breaking news: Earlier today, the billionaire banker, Ethan West, announced his campaign to run for governor of New York. Recently, his company was embroiled in a scandal with college fraud from Langstone University, which was a fake school. We are now live with him in Central Park as he gives a speech with intentions to run as an Independent candidate without help from corporate donations."

I watched the big screen replay my speech from earlier today. I looked at myself, standing with Tim, Garret, and my campaign aides. We were starting out small, but we did get a pretty sizable crowd of about 20,000. I heard a few boos, of course. It was expected, but overall, everyone wanted a picture and a handshake.

My parents couldn't make it because they were out of the country. Once they got back, they'd probably want to get involved. I told them I'd think about it, but I wouldn't be cutting any favors for them or their business friends. The first mistake a lot of people made when running for office was cutting campaign promises. I refused to be indebted to anyone.

The Waldorf Hotel that Genesis rented out was large with black and gold trim surrounding us. It was a ball-room setting with a dance floor with Genesis and Scottie's initials in the middle and large chandeliers hovering above. The staff was all dressed in black and gold suits with the foundation's logo. He invited some of the kids from low-income districts, and Nina had a few people from her community center invited. Tickets to get inside cost fifteen hundred per guest. They also had major artists performing later in the night. What I didn't like and had to get used to was the paparazzi, and the security I had hired once I made the announcement.

A silent auction started the night off. I hated dressing up for these things, but it was for a good cause. Genesis was donating all the money we raised to help support local schools in the communities that had a lack of books, lunches for low-income families, textbooks, and computer equipment.

Genesis, Talbot, and Gage stood next to me in their suits, holding glasses of champagne and joking around. Seeing Talbot dressed up in what he called a "penguin suit" was hilarious. He kept pulling on his tie, and Diya kept slapping his hand down.

"How much longer do we have to do this?" Talbot asked.

"Talbot, we've only been here for thirty minutes," Gage answered.

"The second this is over I'm taking the suit off and burning it," Talbot said.

"Ethan, did you bid on anything?" Diya wondered, looking at the different auction lists on the table.

I nodded and pointed to the signed James Baldwin book that was up for auction at $20,000.

"Nice pick, Talbot auctioned off free tattoos for a year to help raise funds."

"Maya, you look so beautiful!" Nina screeched in

delight as Maya hugged her and gave her an air kiss to avoid getting their makeup messed up.

She was stunningly beautiful in her gown. Her hair was up in curls that dangled loosely down her neck. Her skin glowed in the black dress that was low cut with a long split on the side. "*Damn*," I mumbled to myself.

"Ethan! Ethan!" I heard someone calling my name.

Looking over my shoulder, I saw Hannah striding over with a smirk on her face. Richard was following her. At the same time, Nina was bringing Maya forward.

"You're looking handsome, babe," Hannah said, leaning over to kiss me on the cheek as the camera flashes went off. I smiled, making sure to not alert the media that I really wanted to throw her into a pool of snakes.

"Hannah, how did you get in here?" Scottie demanded aggressively.

Genesis came up behind her to calm her down.

"Who invited you here?" Genesis questioned.

He motioned for security as I stared at Maya willing her to catch my eye. She wouldn't look up from her phone.

"Genesis, you know my family donates to your foundation every year. My parents send their love and I thought it would be nice to come and support my man on his campaign mission."

"I'm good on my own, Hannah. I suggest you leave now before security throws you out."

Right as I finished my comment, security came up to lead them out. Richard walked out like a puppet on a string.

"What did you ever see in her?" Nina asked curiously, taking the glass of champagne out of Gage's hand.

"Don't ask," I said. "Nina, you're looking beautiful and Maya, you look stunning."

"All right, stop flirting with my wife," Gage said.

Nina tugged on his tie to make sure it was straight and kissed him on the lips.

Gage had told me about the time he bid on a date for Nina and then took her to Fiji. They were made for each other, and the time we went out on a date, I could see it in her eyes that she wasn't really into me like that, and I felt the same way. Our relationship was more like friends or siblings. She even asked me if I would be Thalia's godfather, since Genesis and Scottie were Tailynn's godparents, and Diya and Talbot were godparents to their son.

"I think it's time for me to make my announcement. Ethan, you want to join me on stage?" Genesis asked, threading through the crowd as Tim and Garret came behind me.

I wanted to have Maya next to me up there, but I knew making it seem like we had a relationship was foolish, since we still hadn't even had an actual date.

But that would all change tonight.

"Thank you all for coming tonight," Genesis announced. "You know, we have these events every year to help support our community. We can all admit we come from a very privileged place and giving back is something my wife and I are very passionate about. So, along those lines, I decided to do something that I've never done publicly, and this was the perfect time because a good friend of mine is taking on a big role to help the state of New York. With that in mind, I would like to say I wholeheartedly endorse Ethan West as the next governor of New York." Genesis clapped his hands, gesturing for me to come make a speech.

Waving and shaking his hand, I stood in front of the podium as the camera flashes went off.

Out of the corner of my eye, I saw Maya clapping and I winked at her to let her know she was on my radar.

"Thank you, Genesis and Scottie, for graciously letting me steal a little bit of your night. This was a decision I didn't make lightly, but I knew my purpose in life was more than just making money and helping other people become rich. I know the road isn't easy; I mean, look how much the media has hammered on about those photos that were taken while I was in a consensual relationship. Let's get back to what really matters to New Yorkers, and that's better education, healthcare, and affordable housing. She's probably going to yell at me later, but I want to publicly thank Scottie for joining my campaign as a senior advisor. Her knowledge and support are the reason she was picked, on top of her great skills at reading people," I said.

Stepping off the podium, Scottie came over to pose with Genesis and me. The camera flashes went off as each side screamed our names, trying to get us to turn to the left, then the right.

"You think you're slick, making that announcement early," Scottie grumbled under her breath.

"I'm a politician, that's what we do."

Genesis stayed on the podium, answering questions as I walked toward Diya and Maya, who were talking.

"That was a great speech, Ethan! You have my vote!" Diya gleefully cheered.

"Thanks, Diya. What about you, Maya?" I hounded her.

"Good job, Ethan."

"Wow, I'm shocked," I stated.

Talbot spoke in Diya's ear, and she giggled, then stalked off, holding his hand.

As the room grew large with more attendants, I grasped Maya's hand, leading her to the corner hallway.

"You seemed preoccupied earlier when you first walked inside. But then I gave my speech, and you smiled. Now, you're using my first name. I guess I'm finally wearing you down with my charm."

She crossed her arms over her chest.

"I was talking to my sister about my crazy mother when I first got here. Then I saw you had your little girlfriend here, so I didn't want to disturb you," Maya remarked.

"She's not my girlfriend. If I play my cards right, that role will be taken up by Maya Armstrong."

"You're so sure of yourself, Ethan."

I slide my hands in my pocket. "I am."

"Okay."

I stared into her eyes. "Okay what?"

"Let's go," she challenged, tapping her foot.

"To where?"

"Your place, or a hotel. Anywhere. I'm not in the mood to be alone, and you still owe me an interview."

"Maya, what are you saying?" I groaned, leaning in close and placing a hand behind her head to cut the distance between us. I ran my index finger up her arm and down her chest, stopping a few inches from her exposed breasts and tapping her diamond necklace instead.

She stared into my eyes.

A lump formed in my throat.

"I want to fuck, Ethan. Can you do that? Fuck me. Take me to another place, where I'm not the Maya

Armstrong of FBX TV, or Hazel Armstrong's daughter, or Kasey's big sister, or even Nina and Scottie's best friend. Just a night of two consenting adults who find each other attractive and want to explore what those feelings are."

I groaned, bending down, and kissing the top of her forehead and grasping her hand. I didn't answer. Swaggering through the crowd, I just left everyone else behind, not caring if the media saw us leaving together or if Tim had a problem with me leaving and not answering questions.

Tonight, I only wanted to please Maya and let her know she could depend on me.

Chapter 11

Ethan

The elevator stopped at the top penthouse floor. I squeezed her hand, letting her walk off in front of me. Ever since I saw her the first time at Nina's house with her smart-ass mouth, I wanted to give her something to spazz out about, so I could kiss the disrespect away. Then Garret wanted me to do an interview with her. Well, seeing as how she always had a snappy comeback to my questions, tonight, Maya Armstrong would finally have a reason to talk shit.

I made a quick involuntary appraisal of her features. *Damn.* I went back to the door and placed the do not disturb sign and told the security guard I was in for the night. She inhaled sharply at my contact. I squeezed her against me, drinking in her smell, smacking her ass, and pulling back.

A glint of humor ran across her face.

"This is funny to you?"

"What?"

"You really think I can't handle you, Maya?"

She shrugged, walked around me, and headed toward

the bar and I grasped her hand before she could get far. "Take off your dress," I spoke with cool authority.

She bit her lip, slowly and seductively, her gaze slid downward to my dick sitting against her stomach. I watched her intently as she backed up and turned around, unzipping her dress slowly.

I licked my lips taking off my tuxedo jacket and tie.

The dress fell to the floor and she stepped out.

"Stop."

I wanted to look at her for a few more minutes as she stood in her black thong, stockings, and garters. Her strapless bra was holding up the perkiest breasts I'd ever seen.

"Turn around," I ordered.

She turned around and placed her hands on her hips.

"You're beautiful."

"Thank you."

"Now undress me."

Her wide-eyed innocence was merely a smoke screen. I knew Maya was the type of woman that liked to be in control in the bedroom. She finally met her match because I wasn't giving in that easy. I would let this moment linger before I fucked her. I didn't plan on taking her home until the morning.

"Come here." Maya walked over to me swaying her hips. She unbuttoned my shirt buttons one by one, then I stepped out of my shoes as she started to unbuckle my pants. "Bedroom?" she asked.

"Table." I picked her up and carried her over to the glass table in the dining room of the suite. It was the presidential suite equipped with everything like a normal apartment.

"Ooooh. It's cold, Ethan."

"It won't be for long." I walked off toward the kitchen

to grab what I needed. She thought this was going to be a quick fuck. I had something for that ass.

I stepped into the dining room with a tray of ice cubes, whipped cream, strawberries, and chocolate.

"What are you doing?"

"Making a Maya sundae, lean back."

She watched as I spread her thighs wide an instant before I leaned down, taking the ice cube into my mouth. She ran a hand up my chest. I grasped her hand, kissing it, and then her lips. I ran the ice cube across her lips. She tried to take it out of my hands, and I denied her. Already, I could see her getting wet from my refusal to give in to her demands. Cupping her left breast, I pulled her bra down, licking across her tortured, chocolate-brown nipples. She moaned, gripping my hair. I watched as her nipples hardened under the coolness of the ice cube.

She panted in anticipation with lust brimming in her eyes. "Ethan...."

Doing the same thing to her right breast, I added the ice cube across her nipple and then down her chest moving slowly toward her belly button.

She tensed as I swiped my tongue over her needy bud again.

"How do you feel?" I asked.

"Stop torturing me."

"That's not going to happen, baby." I brought the ice cube across her covered pussy and she shivered in response. Shifting, I moved away from the ice cube and slid her thong down. Taking the strawberry, I dipped it in the chocolate. I let her take a bite, which let a small amount of chocolate drizzle down my finger. She gripped my hand and pulled it into her mouth, sucking my finger while keeping her eyes trained on me.

"Shh... you like that."

Picking up the strawberry, I ran it up her inner right and left thighs, then I rubbed it gently around her pussy lips to top it off with her warm juices. I licked up her right thigh, placing small bites as I went. She moaned in pleasure. Doing the same thing to her left thigh, I opened her pussy lips again and took my tongue from her asshole to her bud, and then I stood back up to kiss her lips so she could taste herself and take a bite of the strawberry.

I dropped my pants and boxers and opened the condom and she slid it down my length.

She opened her legs wider and I eased in slowly with just the tip. The warmth was already making me want to burst.

"I don't think I have enough condoms," I muttered to myself, but she overheard and laughed.

"I told you this pussy was life-changing."

I slapped her thigh and eased in farther, and we both gasped at the same time. Her pussy held a death grip on me.

"Maya," I grunted.

"Yes, Mr. West," she moaned, arching her back off the table.

Pulling back out, I thrust again, hitting rock bottom.

"God damn!" I shouted, slapping the table. "Call my name again."

"Mr. West! Oh, Ethan! Right there."

I lifted her off the table with me still inside. I moved us to the bedroom and gently placed her down, never removing myself. Arranging her up close to the headboard, I widened her legs, thrusting, holding one leg in my arm and the back of the headboard with the other as her right leg stretched toward the side in butterfly sign.

"Fuck! Maya... you feel so good, baby."

Wildly, I pumped into her, reveling in the sensations. Our bodies brushed against each other, my heat crashing into hers.

There was no turning back now.

* * *

We went four rounds, and I was completely satisfied with just eating her pussy for the rest of the night, but she ended up falling asleep after our last round, and I didn't want her to be too tired for work the next day. So, I let her sleep and made sure to have a car for her to get home with. I had an early meeting, so I left Maya in bed with the room service I ordered after I showered and dressed.

That was a week ago. Since then, the campaign office had been bustling with our phones ringing off the hook. Genesis's announcement helped to stir up excitement and encouragement for volunteers to come out and help with passing out flyers, going door to door and passing the message along that we're better together.

I ended up working late on the campaign most nights; answering questions, taking calls from reporters, and talking with my lawyer to get Hannah blocked from social media and stop her from following my accounts. She somehow got a lot of celebrity bloggers to do interviews with her, and they posted them all over the internet. My lawyer sent her a cease-and-desist letter, and a defamation lawsuit was pending if she didn't stop. The second Genesis kicked her out of the event, she started going on about how I was corrupt and didn't support her after she lost the baby—a baby she was never pregnant with in the first place. I was starting to think she really lost her mind.

Her parents finally tried to get her to stop, but she was on a mission.

I sat with Tim, and we ran over my schedule for the rest of the month. My office was decorated by my mother, since she wanted to have a hand in something, and I didn't care to argue with her; if it made her happy, then I would rather keep her from going out on her own and starting up some drama that would end up embarrassing me instead.

"You have that meeting with Scottie, another campaign event at Bengals Stadium and if you want to do a few magazine covers, we have *Men of Politics* wanting to sit and do an interview. The owner's cousin ran for mayor and I helped him when he had a scandal and he introduced me to him," Tim said.

"Try to not pack too much in one day, I need to sleep at some point."

"I think the interview you do with Maya will help. Have you set a time and date yet?"

"I've been slammed here and then still finishing up my transition from putting my cousin in the CEO position at the office. That's taking longer than expected because of the red tape with foreign investments," I answered.

My thoughts drifted off to that night with Maya in the hotel, and her cries of pleasure.

I had her climbing the walls ... literally. I had her up against the wall in a split second with her back to me, and I was eating her pussy from behind.

"Ethan!" she cried. "Wait, oh, my God! You're trying to kill me... ooh, shit..."

"I can live in this pussy all night, baby."

"Mmmm... damn you."

"Tell me what you want."

"I want... your... tongue in my ass. Then... I... ugh... shit... I want some dick!"

* * *

"Ethan, are you listening? Ethan?" Tim snapped me out of my trance.

"Sorry, what did you say?"

"I said we got word that your taxes are good and officially on the ballot without any issues, so we're full-force with enough signatures. The minute you can get Maya on board with an interview, that would be great."

"Set it up or have Scottie call her."

"Why can't you call her?"

"It would be better having the campaign office contact her for official political questions."

He wasn't really buying my answer. "Let me guess, you slept with her and haven't called, am I right?"

"Just make the call, Tim."

Chapter 12

Maya

"Maya! Maya!"

I was sitting inside Jane's Bistro with Emery, Scottie, Diya, and Nina. We were catching up since the last time we were all together at the fundraiser. It had been one week since I saw Ethan, and he hadn't called. I didn't know whether I should be thankful or pissed off. I was usually the one who did the dumping after a quick fuck. Not the other way around.

"Huh."

"What's wrong with you?" Diya picked a pickle off my plate.

"Nothing."

"Macy's is having a 40% off sale."

I checked my phone to see if anyone texted me. "That's nice."

A fork slammed on the table. I looked up, and all six eyes were on me. "What?"

"Maya, you've never been quiet, so tell us what's going on with you," Emery demanded, grabbing another lemonade from the waitress.

"All right if I tell you, don't say anything to your men. I mean it, Nina."

She pointed at herself in disbelief.

"Yep. You're the first one who will run to Gage and tell him all of my business."

"I do not. That's Emery."

"Nina, don't fall for the redirect. Maya, tell us what's going for real. Are you pregnant?" Scottie inquired.

"No. Why is that the first thing everyone wants you to say when you have to have a serious conversation?"

My phone buzzed again, and I saw a news alert that Ethan was having a town hall meeting at the public library. A second alert came through that showed a blurry photo of him with a woman, and she was on her knees in front of him.

I dropped the glass of lemonade in my hand, my face twisted in shock. "That bastard."

"What bastard?" Emery grabbed my phone out of my hands.

"Oh."

"Let me see," Nina shouted. "Damn, Ethan," Nina shouted.

"Are you two?"

I smoothed my hair down. "Ummm, we kind of slept together."

"Kind of? How do you 'kind of' sleep with someone?" Diya wondered.

"It was the night of the fundraiser," I muttered, biting my lip to stifle a grin.

"Was he good?" Scottie asked.

I leaned back and closed my eyes in remembrance.

"It was *that* good?" Diya responded and threw a napkin at me, giggling.

I burst out in laughter, and we high-fived each other.

"Mind-blowing and I hate it."

"So, Mr. Stuffy Suit has Maya intrigued?"

"No, Emery. Maya Armstrong is not easily intrigued by any man." I was lying to myself and to my friends. This man was ridiculously sexy, rich, and demanding, with a big dick, and he knew what to do with it. It had me wanting to have a baby, and I was not the type of woman who wanted a baby off some good dick.

"I'm helping him on his campaign," Scottie advised.

"Since when do you work on political campaigns?" I waved the waitress over to order again. "Can I get a scotch on the rocks please?"

"Uh, ma'am, we don't sell liquor here, and it's eleven in the morning," the waitress told me.

"Ugh. Fine."

"Girl, you're just like Nicole right now. Crazy over a man. Do you really like Ethan like that, I mean wanting to date and make him your boyfriend?" Nina leaned on the table speaking in a broken whisper. The restaurant wasn't too crowded, but I appreciated her being discreet with my business.

"I just want sex."

"Okay, well, don't you already do that with Douglas?"

"He can give me oral sex. The things I did with Ethan-- I can't explain it. And to make it worse, he hasn't called me since that one time."

"I see now. You're pissed he did what you normally do to men after you have sex. Kick them out and don't call." Nina's phone vibrated. She picked it up, returning the text message and placed it back down. "Gage," she said to our unasked question.

"Are the kids good?" I inquired.

"Yeah, Tailynn wants to know what time we are going to Gage's game later today. You want to tag along?"

"No, I have something I have to do tonight."

He thought he was God's gift to women. I'm perfectly capable of not having feelings.

* * *

Telling myself I wasn't really feeling him was a lie within itself. The things he did to my body I couldn't describe. I was sitting here on a date with this guy named Chuck that I met at the bank the other day. He was average, about five-nine and worked in construction. He wasn't married and I needed to preoccupy my mind with someone else to help me forget that jackass, Ethan.

We'd agreed on a lunch date instead of dinner because tonight I needed to get to bed early. Tomorrow, I had an interview with Ethan that my office organized. This would be the first time we saw each other since that night, and I wanted to really hammer his ass. At the same time, I couldn't let my personal feelings get involved.

"So, Maya, I have to confess your beauty is very overwhelming. I'm really surprised you're not married already," Chuck said.

"I never plan on getting married. I like the way things are with dating on and off."

"Normally women want a ring, house, and kids. My goal is to retire with a wife and kids. Hate to get involved only to have you not be on the same page as me," Chuck said, enveloping my hand.

"Where are you from again?"

He smiled. "The South, baby, born and raised."

"What do you think about Ethan West running for governor?"

"Who?"

"You want to think about marriage and kids, but don't even know the current political climate which would dictate how you live and work, depending on who you vote for? If you can't tell me the policies that he's running on, then how can I have you lead a household as my husband?"

"I-"

I motioned for him to not finish his answer and grabbed my purse and keys, standing up to leave.

"Save it. Thanks again for lunch. Maybe you should focus on a woman that doesn't mind staying quiet and letting you run things. We both know that'll never happen with me."

Strolling out of Jane's, I put my shades back on and walked toward my car. Seeing a billboard for Ethan, I decided to take a little detour before heading home. Sitting in my car across from his office, it was about seven in the evening, not too dark when a knock on my door startled me.

"Thanks for coming," I murmured as Scottie got into the passenger seat.

"Of course, I've been there, lovesick over a guy, before. I know all the steps of trying to avoid your feelings," Scottie said, passing me a pair of binoculars.

"What's this for?"

"To see who's coming and going. I brought some snacks, and I told Genesis I would be here with you for a few hours until you're ready to go inside or go home."

"What if I want to come here tomorrow? I mean the asshole hasn't called me for a week. We had sex one time and he knows he stamped his name on it and now I can't think of anything else but his dumb face." I groaned in frustration, leaning my head back on the seat.

"I can do this all night, honey. You know, Nina and Diya would think this is extreme, but sometimes, you need to just have a moment of craziness—even if it means stalking."

"I'm not stalking him."

"Maya, you're sitting in your car across the street from his campaign office with binoculars and eating Pringles chips listening to Anita Baker. What would you call it?"

"I love Anita Baker."

"I love her too, but sweetie, you're stalking and in love."

"Maya Armstrong does not fall in love."

"The second Maya Armstrong talks in third person, it's time to realize she's in love," she said, passing me the bag of Skittles.

Chapter 13

Maya

The next day, I pulled into the station. Douglas had managed to annoy me into doing this interview with Ethan.

"All right, Maya, remember—this interview can make or break your show. It will determine whether it gets picked up for another season. Make sure to bring up the nude photos and videos that were leaked. This could be great, Maya."

I checked my makeup one more time as I went over my notes for the interview with Ethan. The other night ran through my mind and I needed to stay focused and not let my judgment get clouded with his sexy lies. That bastard was probably engaged for real. I'm making a fool of myself running up behind him, it's changing me from the Maya Armstrong I was born to be.

"I'm so jealous of you, Maya, you get to interview with Ethan West. I swear if I had five minutes alone with him, ooh child," Keisha, my cousin and the lead hairdresser, joked.

"Ouch, too tight."

"Sorry."

"That man is not worried about you, Keisha. Don't let that Public Relations girl hear you lusting about her man."

She blew a breath of annoyance. "That little skinny stick couldn't hold that man's interest for too long. I heard she's the one that's sending all those nude photos to the media."

"I don't buy it. He's still seeing her probably."

"Huh."

I pulled back squinting my eye at her. "What's that huh for?"

"You seem really upset at him and the PR girl supposedly dating."

"I'm not upset."

"Could have fooled me."

"I have no idea what you're talking about." Right now, I was in denial about the emotions that had been coursing through me since seeing the latest picture.

"Says the woman that's wearing a too tight blouse showing off her cleavage, and thigh high stockings with a pencil skirt so tight she can barely walk. I'm going to mind my business," Keisha teased.

"Whose side are you on?"

Amusement crossed her face. "Yours, cousin, but it doesn't mean I won't keep it real with you. Now, tell me— how was he in bed?"

"None of your business."

Someone knocked on my door and came inside.

"Maya, are you ready? I have Ethan and his team here on set," Douglas said, holding the door open.

"Yes," I said, standing and doing one more check of my makeup. I had the wardrobe stylist pick out a light pink dress shirt with ankle boots, and a gold necklace and ring that made the entire outfit pop on camera. The PA passed me the cue cards, and I followed Douglas to the set.

Keisha was touching up Ethan's makeup. I strolled to my seat opposite him. Whenever I had one-on-one interviews, I used a simple couch and side table with my logo in the background.

"How are you, Maya?" Ethan asked.

I had to keep my emotions in check. "I'm good, Mr. West, thank you for coming."

"We're back to that again?" Ethan replied.

Ignoring his question, I watched as the camera team started getting things in place.

"Mr. West, I want you to know you have my vote," Keisha remarked, stepping out of frame and standing next to Larry.

"Thank you, Keisha," Ethan said.

Amused, she let a sneaky smile spread across her face.

"5, 4, 3, 2... you're live," my executive producer told me through the earpiece.

"Welcome to *Spotlight with Maya Armstrong*. I'm your host, Maya. The blogger, stylist, and celebrity tea spiller that keeps you up to date. Today's a little different because we have an exclusive sit-down interview with the Independent candidate for Governor of New York, Ethan West. Thank you, Mr. West, for agreeing to sit down and discuss your plans," I opened, turning from the face of the camera to Ethan, giving him eye contact.

He smiled and nodded in answer.

"I believe this is your first stop on your campaign trail, so I know my viewers are very excited to see you on our little show, and how you will deal with the issues that affect regular people every day."

"I look forward to discussing many things with you, Maya," Ethan stated, leaning back in his seat, and opened his suit jacket. I attempted to focus, evaluating his body language and nice demeanor. He was testing me.

I cleared my throat. "So, you officially kicked everything off at Central Park. How was that experience, and what made you want to run for governor? Why not mayor or city councilman?"

"Central Park was great; I really connected with my supporters—and even the protestors. Listen, there will always be a difference of opinion on certain ways of getting things done in our community. I admit my privilege and where I came from. You'll never catch me apologizing for making money. I was given something from my grandfather, and I tripled it, and I use it in ways that don't only help myself. Also, I improve the lives of my employees at all my branches, and the charities I've helped by donating to and investing in. As a matter of fact, a mutual friend of ours, Nina Mitchell, had a community center that was on the brink of getting sold. I approached her about what I could do to help, and she accepted. She turned it around and opened other centers."

"What are your plans for the first ninety days if you get into office?"

"The first ninety days I want to do an overhaul of housing, freeze rent hikes, and build more hotels."

"Do you think you'll have the support of both sides of the aisle once you get in office?"

"We won't know until I get in office."

"On that note, we'll take a break and be right back with more questions for Ethan West." I smiled, pointing my cue cards up, and the red light went off, showing we were no longer airing.

I stood up about to walk off to get a touch up when Ethan jumped up reaching for my hand. I turned glancing at his hand.

"Can we talk?" Ethan asked.

Removing his hand, I motioned for Keisha to give me a second. "Talk."

"Not here. Let me officially take you out to eat."

"No, thank you. I wouldn't want your girlfriend thinking you're involved with me."

"Girlfriend?"

"Yes. Hannah, right? The fiancée."

Making a noise in his throat, he growled out, "Maya."

"Ten seconds!" the executive producer shouted.

"We have a show to finish," I responded, pressing my lips together to fight wanting to jump his bones. I needed to stay focused.

"Mr. West, you have recently received the endorsements of Genesis Maguire and Scottie Maguire. Scottie is working as your senior campaign manager, am I correct?"

"Genesis and I go way back, and I met Scottie through him. She's extremely smart, funny, and knows what is going on in the community. I wanted people around me who aren't afraid to tell me when I'm wrong."

"I agree. You're actually going to answer town hall like questions from the blog readers if I'm not mistaken," I stated.

"My campaign manager, Tim, got me some time to answer a few questions. Scottie was gracious enough to be the point person on canvassing through the mail that was sent in, and I'm scheduled to go there sometime this week."

"Before we let you go, I have a few fantasy fast questions to ask that all my guests have to answer in six seconds without thinking too hard about your answer."

"Go ahead."

"Favorite vacation spot?"

"Italy."

"Favorite celebrity crush?"

"She wouldn't want me to say her name publicly, but her first initial starts with an M," he teased, licking his lips.

"Favorite dessert?"

"You..."

"Thank you again, Mr. West, for sitting with me today and answering my questions. We've run over, and I know you have to get back to work on your campaign. Good luck, and we wish you well," I said, cutting him off from saying what I thought he was going say. I didn't want him telling my personal business to the world, which is probably why I didn't ask him about the photos or Hannah.

He winked right as the music started, and the red light went off. His team came over and shook hands with me, and I thanked them for coming but didn't stay to hear him out. I left to go home, open a bottle of wine, and soak in the tub.

* * *

I was preparing to meet Douglas for dinner to celebrate the early numbers from viewership. He'd invited Tonya and a few crew members from the show. But somehow, they all declined, according to him. Douglas probably figured I was dumb and would fall for the last-minute cancellation act ... and then fall into his lap for sex.

"I saw your interview today with Ethan. It looked intense," Nina said over the FaceTime call.

Running a towel over my arm, I listened to the kids screaming in the background as I sipped on my glass of Moscato. "He did all right."

"Where are you going tonight? No, Thalia, put that down. Gage, can you please watch your daughter and stop rubbing my leg?" Nina snapped, while Gage tried to flirt with her.

"Leave my little baby doll alone. She's not hurting anybody. Ain't that right, Thalia? Give Daddy a kiss," I overheard Gage say.

"She's so cute. We need to have an auntie-and-niece day," I said, grinning at Gage and Nina's daughter.

Thalia tried reaching for the phone, and Nina kissed her cheek. When Nina pulled back, Gage grasped the back of her head and planted a long, enduring kiss on her lips.

"Ew... take that somewhere else," I complained.

Gage flipped me off and walked away with Thalia in his arms.

"Leave my man alone and figure out your own game plan to get Ethan back."

"Anyway. I want to do another girls' night with you guys. Everyone's so busy and I'm missing our popcorn and wine night."

She walked into the kitchen and opened the fridge grabbing a bottle of water. "That would be fun. Text me the time and day."

"I can hear the music playing in the background.

Sounds like a Barney festival.. Let me get off this phone, so I can meet up with Douglas," I said, hanging up.

I shuffled out of the bathroom, dried off, and removed the towel from my head. Shaking it out, I grabbed a brush and combed it into a high ponytail. Picking up the outfit that I'd laid out earlier, I slid on my one-piece jumper and gold belt. I lightly dabbed on foundation and lip gloss. Douglas would not get the full treatment tonight. Spraying the latest JLo perfume on, I searched for my gold clutch purse and my keys.

I'd scheduled a limo service earlier, and it was right on time as I closed the door and locked up. Heading to the car, I slid inside and smiled as the driver pulled away.

Chapter 14

Ethan

The city lights were beautiful through the hotel window. I could still smell her scent lingering around me. I sipped on a shot, letting it run down my throat and turn my blood hot. I recalled Maya's moans and cries as I thrust into her sweet, tight pussy. I wanted another night with her, but after the debacle with Hannah, I didn't want another woman trying to force herself into my life.

I heard familiar laughter and turned to see the one woman I couldn't keep my thoughts and dreams from lingering on coming up to the table.

"Ethan, how are you?" Douglas held his hand out for me to shake.

I grinned, noticing Maya looking around and avoiding eye contact with me, and returned Douglas's handshake. "I'm good, Douglas. Maya."

"Ethan."

"I hope we aren't on your bad side after the interview Maya did earlier. I'd hate to have the future governor censoring our station," Douglas said, quirking one eyebrow inquisitively.

She hugged her arms to herself.

"I think Maya did a fantastic job."

"Thank you, Ethan," she said, taking a sip of her wine.

Douglas looked between us as my eyes stayed on her face. I wanted her lips wrapped around my dick, taking my seed down her throat.

"Are you two on a date?" I questioned, taking a seat, not caring if I was interrupting.

"Yes."

"No." They both answered at the same time.

Douglas cleared his throat.

"We're celebrating the interview; the rest of the team is coming," Maya expressed.

"So, my team and I can join you. They're meeting me right now, actually. You don't mind, do you, Douglas?" I pressed, imposing myself on their impromptu date.

Tim and Scottie walked up right as the server came over to give me a menu. But I wasn't really hungry for food tonight. "Scottie, thank you for coming tonight," I greeted her, standing to pull her chair out for her.

"Maya, you looked amazing earlier today. And tonight, you're showing off again," Scottie gushed.

Tim reached out and shook Douglas's hand and hugged Maya before sitting.

"I guess it's a party now," Douglas said snidely.

"Hello, I'm Kevin," the waiter interrupted. "I'll be your server tonight. Can I get you three something to drink?"

"Actually, what I want isn't on the menu. You can bring me a shot of Hennessey," I demanded, watching Maya avoid my eyes.

"Kevin, can you bring the table a round of champagne on me?" Douglas insisted.

"Maya, we wanted to know if traveling while you're filming your talk show will be a hindrance to you," Tim wondered.

"Douglas is willing to work around my schedule, so I can pre-tape earlier and spread it out over the few weeks I'm away, following the trail," Maya responded.

"We didn't talk about you doing this full-time," Douglas whispered, trying not to appear embarrassed.

"Remember, my contract states I can do outside projects if I can accommodate the show taping," Maya spat.

"Maya, let's discuss this later," Douglas snidely commented.

The server took Scottie's order, then Tim's, and shuffled away.

"Ethan, tomorrow we're meeting at my office and Genesis told me to tell you if you need him at any of your rallies to just call him," Scottie said.

"I'll call him to thank him for all of his help. He even offered to handle the Hannah situation. But her parents are finally taking her seriously and since the interview aired earlier today, I've been getting calls left and right, and endorsements from people that at first wanted me to drop out because they felt I was tainted," I said.

We continued discussing my upcoming events as Kevin brought Scottie and Tim's food out.

* * *

One hour later I was walking out of the hotel restaurant with Maya beside me.

"How long are you going to ignore me?"

"One week."

"What?" I questioned, her two-word answer baffling me.

"We slept together, and you left the next morning with not so much as a thank-you note. Then I don't hear from you until today at the studio. So, please excuse me if I've ignored your precious feelings. But you only get one chance with Maya Armstrong, and you sir, have played all your cards."

"Nina told me about you talking in third person when you get really excited about something or extremely pissed. Forgive me please," I pleaded, remorseful, running a finger across her bottom lip.

"No thanks, and I'll see you when I report for duty at the office," she said, attempting to walk around me.

"Where are you going?"

"Home."

"What can I do to get you to forgive me?"

* * *

"Oh... yes. Eat this pussy, Ethan."

She was fully aware of the hardness in my pants. Her moans and groans pierced my soul as I lapped at her juices.

"Keep going... shit!"

The degree to which she responded to my tongue entering her asshole drove me to go faster.

"Oh, my God! Ethan!" she shouted, gripping the sheets as she came for the second time. She writhed until her orgasm came down.

I stood, undoing my shirt. But the next words out of her mouth made me freeze.

"I don't have time for that. Thanks for the head though." She rolled off the bed grabbing her clothes and getting dressed.

"Maya, you can't leave me like this," I said, pointing down to my dick poking through my pants.

"Watch me," she snipped, checking her hair in the mirror, smirking, and walking out of my hotel room.

Chapter 15

Ethan

I was sitting with Scottie in her office, going through the questions for the column.

"So, you're going to answer some questions that people sent in, and then we'll go from there."

"Thanks for doing this, Scottie. Genesis told me you're the best, and your honesty will help."

"No problem, has Hannah come to any of your campaign events?"

My voice was heavy with sarcasm. "I found out from Tim's assistant, Garret, that she tried to get tickets to the next town hall meeting I'm throwing at Talbot's shop."

She leaned back in her chair, relaxing. "What about Maya?"

"Maya?"

I knew she wasn't going to make this easy on me. I found it amusing it took this long for her friend to ask me about her.

"Don't play coy with me, Ethan, I set you up with Nina and Gage almost bit my head off. Now you find yourself in bed with her friend after the auction."

The wide smile tipped the corners of my mouth thinking about my night with Maya Armstrong. "Nina and I are friends. Gage and I are friends, we both knew from the moment we met it was only friendship and nothing more. Now the reason I'm here is to talk about the constituents. You know I don't kiss and tell. If I pursue anything with Maya, you'll be the second person behind Maya that will know."

"So, are you planning on pursuing Maya?"

I groaned picking up the first letter addressed to Scottie's forum. Scottie slapped my hand away.

"Don't touch. This is my job, Mr. Candidate."

"Which we both can agree on, so...can we get started on you doing your job?"

"Someone's a jerk," Scottie scoffed, opening the first letter.

Reader "Media Student": *Dear Mr. West, thank you for taking our questions. This is something we haven't seen from a candidate before, and we appreciate you taking the time to get to know the people. My question is about education. I'm a college student, studying media and journalism. I work a full-time job and still can't afford all my books and classes. What are your plans for making college affordable?*

"Great question," Scottie stated.

"It is, how many do you normally get a week?"

"Mostly fifty to a hundred a week. Since we announced this special edition version with you, I guess it opened up the door for a flood of questions. You don't have to answer them all," Scottie insisted.

Candidate Corner: *Thank you for sending in your question. I want to first say thank you to "Scottie" for allowing me to impose upon her readers with my answers. To answer your question, I am confident in my plans to lower taxes for the middle class, which will make classes more affordable and open more avenues for students to afford books, room, and board.*

"Great answer, I'll type this up and mail them all off together."

Reader "Surviving Housing": *Mr. West, what are you going to do about the housing crisis in New York? I'm a mother of four kids and work two jobs. I still struggle with paying for childcare, food, clothes, sending my kids to a decent public school, and living in a three-bedroom rental with two baths.*

Candidate Corner: *Thank you for taking the time out of your day to send in your question. My plans for the housing crisis are to put into place a bill that will stop the rise in cost for the next three years on rent fees. I have a team in place to look into the costs and affordability of fixing up lower income apartments first and then homes.*

We want the government to work for you and not against your growth in living and raising your family without going into debt.

"She's brave for putting herself out there with this question. I mean, we don't get millions of papers sold, but with you answering these questions, our numbers for this edition will pick up," Scottie said.

"Can you get her contact information so I can have someone get in touch with her? I want to personally send her some help."

"Sure, and I think it can help your campaign." Scottie nudged me in the shoulder. That wasn't why I wanted to do it; I've always helped those who needed it. But if it helped the campaign in some way, I'd take it as a side benefit.

Reader "Undecided Voter": *Mr. West, I believe you want to help rebuild New York toward the future, I'm an undecided voter. Tell me why I should vote for you over the other candidates?*

Candidate Corner: *Thank you, Undecided Voter, for writing into the column today. The future of New York is dependent on the people, and who they vote for. Not only for the governorship, but for the lower city council, the education department, the mayor, and more policies that are on the ballot. I want to earn your vote by working with* *you. I want to be transparent and put every bill that is brought to my desk online for the people to see. The problem we have right now is that money is being spent with nothing to show for it, and I intend to stop the bleeding. I've maintained my wealth by being smart with how and where I spend my money, and the investments I choose. We aren't choosing wisely as a city, and we need everyone on board to change that.*

"How about another one before you leave?" Scottie asked.

"I'm game."

Reader "Single and Free": *Mr. West, I don't have a major question, but my daughter is divorced and single. Are you dating anyone right now? Because she'd be perfect for you.*

Scottie and I burst into laughter at the question.

Candidate Corner: *Single and Free, I'm flattered, but at the moment the campaign is my girlfriend. Tell your daughter she's lucky to have you looking out for her."*

"Good job, Ethan. I'll have this sent out tomorrow. What do you have for the rest of the day?"

"I have to go see my parents, they're back in town. Then I'll be meeting with my cousin to finish signing the paperwork."

"You really signed off to give your company over to your cousin? I commend you for really sticking to your principles and not being like the other money hungry politicians in this city."

"It was hard, because I can be a little anal about how things are going. I can't say I won't give advice from time to time. Overall, I trust him to lead the way. The good thing is when I win the governorship, and he fucks up, I'll fire his ass and find someone else to run it successfully."

"I'm surprised Richard and Cody haven't tried to work with Hannah."

I rose up taking my vibrating phone out of my pocket.

"Genesis is helping me monitor Richard, along with Cody. I never let an enemy think they have me backed into a corner. Cody's not stupid. If he really wants to make a move to take over my company, he'll have to kill me first. Hannah is a puppet, and Richard is too dumb to realize he's on his way to jail right after her," I replied confidently.

I saw a message from my mother on my phone.

Mom: What time are you coming over?

Me: Now. Give me 10 minutes.

"Thanks again, Scottie. So, I'll see you at Talbot's shop, right, for our next event?" I questioned.

Standing, she straightened her shoulders and cleared her throat, extending her hand for me to shake. "Senior

Advisor to the Governor of New York, reporting for duty," Scottie answered.

* * *

I parked in front of the newest mansion my family had bought. The massive, modern, three-story home was over 30,000 square feet with eight bedrooms, ten bathrooms, a tennis court, an indoor spa, and many other luxuries they never had time to take in because they loved to travel in the 2020 Bentley my father had bought as an anniversary present.

My childhood home, which we still had, was a Georgian-style mansion, but once I went off to college, they didn't stay in one place for too long. My mother loved showing off to her friends and buying the most expensive house on the block. That was her idea of being the Joneses—even though, at one point, I had to financially help them.

Shutting the door and heading inside, I saw my mother sitting on the couch. She was talking on the phone and watching the latest celebrity gossip show on TV. Scoping out the room, I didn't see my father around.

"Oh, he's here, Margaret. Let me call you back... okay, lunch tomorrow. I have to show you the new mink fur I got," my mother said, hanging up. She stood to hug and kiss me on the cheek.

"Hello, son. You're looking well," she commented.

I sat down next to her on the couch, and stated, "I am. What did you need to meet with me about?"

"Well, I wanted to first apologize for how I behaved with the Hannah situation, and your father is sorry for how things turned out. She was the first woman you brought home to us and we became friends with her family. I guess we became attached and wanted you with her at your own expense."

"Has she been around here lately?"

"I do still talk with her parents, but they understand she can't come here anymore."

"I appreciate the support; I wish it had come sooner, before things got ugly. The media has slowed down after my lawyer sent a lawsuit threat for reposting the nude photos."

"Why would she have nude photos of you anyway?"

"Mom. I'm not talking about this with you."

"I know how it is when you're young and in love, but I never did anything like that," she expressed.

"Uhm...anyway, where's Dad?"

She shook her head disapprovingly. "Somewhere with his golf buddies."

"I wanted to invite you to Talbot's tattoo shop. I'm having a small gathering with a few supporters."

"How is Talbot doing?"

"He's great, and Genesis endorsed my campaign."

"That's wonderful, son. I need to go check in on Mi-Mi. We talked over the phone. Now that I'm back in town, I need to go visit her. The kids are getting so big. When are you going to give me some grandkids?"

"Let me win the nomination first. Then we can talk about kids in about ten years."

"Ten years! Ethan, you're moving into the type of lifestyle that's highly scrutinized. A single guy would not be looked upon as favorable. You need a wife and kids immediately. Is there anybody you're interested in?" she queried.

Her mentioning a wife and kids reminded me of

Maya and how we've played this cat and mouse game between us.

"Mi-Mi would love a visit from you, and I know the opening game of the baseball season is this month, and everyone is going, plus the kids. So, you should see if Dad is interested," I explained, changing the subject.

She wrinkled her nose and shook her head. "What should I wear to the baseball game? I mean, Chanel wouldn't look good because those seats are so small, and my Alexander McQueen coat needs the perfect lighting to get the entire effect."

"Gage normally gets the box for the entire family. If you want to come, let me know. I need to head out to go over some last-minute things for West Bank and Investments. Tell Dad I said hello when he comes back, and I'll have a car sent for you if you decide to come to the game," I suggested, getting up, turning on my heels, and striding to the door to leave.

Chapter 16

Maya

Three nights later

"Diya... he saw me on a date with Douglas. That asshole is playing games."

"You sound conflicted," Diya replied.

I laid up with the girls having a sleepover. We were wearing our pajamas, drinking wine, eating popcorn, and catching up on our lives.

Nicole couldn't make it this time because of her DJ gig tonight.

"How about we go to the club that Nicole is playing at tonight? I don't have to worry about the kids and Nina, you need a break from Gage. I'm surprised you're not pregnant again," Scottie spoke in her casual, jesting way.

* * *

Later that night, Emery and Scottie came with me to spy on Ethan again.

"Maya, how many times do I have to tell you that this is crazy?" Nina asked over speaker phone. "And Emery, why are you encouraging this?"

"All we're doing is making sure he's not having any women come into his office for a late-night sex romp," I explained.

Nina chuckled. "He's a grown man; he can do what he wants. And you're just drunk off the multiple orgasms he gave you."

I sighed in exasperation.

"Who's that?" Emery asked, pointing at a woman walking toward Ethan's office door.

"Nina, I have to go." I hung up before she could reply. Grabbing the binoculars, I leaned closer to the window and noticed it was Ethan's ex, Hannah.

"What is she doing here? Are they still dating, Scottie?"

"From what he told me they've been broken up for over two years and she recently started coming around more and leaked those nude photos and video of him."

"That bitch," I spat, trying to open the car door to get out.

"Nope, you stay in this car," Emery said, pulling me back into the car.

We watched as her hands flailed around in front of the door as one of his aides tried to keep her from getting inside.

"Ugh. I hate you," I told Emery.

"Oooh, look, he finally came to the door," Scottie said.

The exchange between them seemed mild, compared to how she was acting when the aide was trying to get her to leave. Her hair was all over the place, and she looked like she hadn't slept in a few days. A car pulled up with its high beams on, and we sunk down, so as not to be seen while still checking out what was going on. Two large men in white scrubs got out of the car and picked her up. She was screaming and kicking as they took her to the car.

"Wow! He really called and got her locked up," I whispered, under my breath.

The door closed and he went back inside and started talking to the same worker that she was arguing with. He grabbed his coat and started to leave right back out the door when someone knocked on my car window scaring the shit out of us.

Rolling the window down he opened the container and pulled a pizza box out.

"Delivery."

"I didn't order this."

"What kind of pizza is it?" Emery asked.

I glared at her question. "Emery, we didn't order this. Sorry, sir, we can't take the pizza."

"Ma'am, I was instructed to give this to a Maya Armstrong sitting out in a car."

My mouth dropped open at his description.

"I hope he included breadsticks," Emery echoed.

"Emery!"

"What? I'm hungry."

I grumbled, taking the pizza out of his hands right as Ethan came outside smirking at us as he swaggered to his car.

"He knows," I fumed.

I paid the delivery driver with an extra $20 tip. We drove off, and I watched as Emery started dancing in her seat, taking a bite out of the meat lover's pizza.

"This is so good," Emery cheerfully clapped.

"Friends don't let friends eat pizza from the enemy," I fussed.

"The same enemy that had you screaming his name and you've been lovesick ever since."

"Whose side are you on?" I insisted, folding my arms over my chest leaning back into the window waiting for an answer.

"The right side. As your friend, I will always keep it real with you. Same with Nina, Diya, and Nicole—whenever she finally commits to something. You need to realize you have feelings for this man, and the childish games need to stop," Scottie told me.

"I hate when you're right."

"Don't worry, Genesis says the same thing."

We both burst into laughter at her comment.

She parked in front of my home and I started grabbing my things to get out.

"You need to have a conversation with him, Maya. I'm working on his campaign, and I think he can make real changes when he gets in office. Don't be afraid to step out on faith. He's what you need, and I can tell the little wall you have up is coming down. You can't continue to let the pain from your parents' relationship spill over into whatever happiness you come across with Ethan. The two large egos that you both have won't survive. One has to compromise."

"Is that what happened with you and Genesis? One of you compromised?"

She sighed, staring out of the window. "Every relationship is different. You can't compare what we have to what you could potentially have with Ethan. All men aren't the same. I will say that you have to be sure of yourself and know your worth, and what you won't allow. At the same time, don't let him chase you too easily. Make him work for it," Scottie said, with a slow, secret smile, and I understood.

Waving goodbye, I walked into my house and dropped my bag on the floor. Kicking off my shoes, I stumbled into my bedroom, still in my clothes. Not caring about changing, I collapsed onto the bed and fell into a deep sleep.

Ethan

Present

She thought I didn't notice her, always parked outside around this time with her friends. I called Genesis earlier when I was in my office to ask about them always sitting outside.

"What the hell is your problem?"

"Excuse me?" I asked, one eyebrow raised.

I leaned back in my chair crossing my hands on my chest. She was standing in front me wearing black leggings and a crop top without a bra. It was pissing me off that she came out of the house dressed like that.

"All right, let's get this over with because I know I was the best sex you ever had, and you were pretty decent for me."

A grin overtook my features at her admission.

"Pretty decent."

"Fine, you blew my fucking mind, Ethan West. Okay? What do you want me to do? Scream it to the world or something?"

"Under normal circumstances, I would say yes. But with me running for governor, I don't think that would look good."

She blew out an aggravated breath. Finally looking around my office, she stated, "I like your office."

"Thanks," I responded.

"Are you always this hard?" Maya sassed.

I smirked at her comment. She raised her hand to stop me from responding. "I didn't mean it like that," she exclaimed.

I stood and came around the desk. I pointed to the sofa for her to have a seat. She sat with a stern-faced expression. Biting back my wanting to suck on her sexy neck, I sat down next to her with my arm resting on the back of the couch.

"You looked cute in your little MacGyver investigative setup in front of my office for the past few months."

"How did you know?"

I threw my head back and roared in laughter. "Maya, not a lot of people have a pink Audi with the nameplate 'MayaA.' It was pretty obvious. The second all this stuff started with Hannah, I had security monitor my home and offices. They took photos of you, and I told them to leave you alone."

"So, the watcher has been watched?" Her eyes were sharp and assessing me for an answer.

"Something like that."

As she rubbed a hand up her thigh, I felt the need to have her close to me. Picking her up, I turned her around to straddle my lap.

"Ethan! What if someone comes in here?"

"They know to knock first."

"Oh."

"I like you, Maya, and you seem to not take my shit like other women. I can't promise I'll always remember the little things—especially if I win the nomination. I honestly can't tell you the last time I've gone on a date besides our encounter at the charity auction. Can I say I apologize for not staying with you the next morning? It wasn't my intent to make you feel less than. Growing up with parents who weren't the most affectionate or good at staying in one place, I learned to be on-the-go and not get too close to anyone."

"We do have that in common."

"What?"

"Lingering issues from our childhood. I grew up with a father who loved my mother more than himself. She then cheated on him and had a child outside their marriage. She has always tried to control my life, and I pushed back. I didn't care that my father forgave her and wanted to keep his family together. Deep down, I wish he would have divorced her and took us away because she's never been the Mother of the Year. Hell, the other day, she slapped me in the face."

She tugged at my tie. "Parents sometimes show you they're human and not perfect."

"Do you have any siblings?" she asked.

"No, but I'm close to my cousin. He's taking over my business."

"I have a younger sister, Kasey Hughes. She works as a librarian."

"I'd like to meet her one day."

A strange, faintly eager look flashed in her eyes.

"I'm not having sex with you in my office." I playfully kissed her lips, mocking the pout she wore on her face.

"Where do you live?" she inquired.

I chuckled at the twenty questions. "Are we having an interview or getting to know each other?" My voice was low and smooth. I gripped her around the waist and pulled her in close.

She moaned, nuzzling her nose in my neck.

"I haven't decided yet." She had a low, silvery voice.

A knock at my door interrupted us.

"Come in," I called out.

It was my assistant, Carol. When I made my bid for governor known, she wanted to work alongside me on the campaign, instead of staying at the company. "Sir, we have the guest list for the town hall meeting at Talbot's tattoo shop. Security has canvassed and given the all-clear to get started on decorating," Carol stated. She laid the papers on my desk, then turned to Maya. "Hi, I'm Carol. And you must be Maya?"

Maya reached out and captured her hand, trying to get off my lap.

"Ethan, you have company." Maya scowled.

"Don't mind me," Carol said.

"What if it was someone else? I don't want everyone to know I was sitting in the governor's lap."

"First off, I'm not the governor yet. And second, I knew Carol was coming in because I asked for the list before you barged into my office. Thanks, Carol."

"Huh."

"I like her," Carol said.

"You said the same thing about..."

Maya cut me off before I could finish my statement. "If you want to continue getting what's between my legs, you won't speak that person's name in my presence."

Carol chortled, walking out of my office, and closing the door.

"You win." I gave in, kissing the back of her hand.

"Changing the subject, thanks again for letting me follow you as you were going through the debates and town halls. This will really help put my show on the map even more."

"You're welcome, but I'd rather talk about what you're wearing. I didn't say anything at first but looking at you is causing what's in my pants to stir."

She rubbed up and down my third leg and I groaned, stopping her from unzipping my pants.

"I've always wanted to have my Monica moment."

Maya and I burst out laughing.

"Next time. We need to get going because I know Talbot is going crazy with all those people running in and out of his place. Rain check?"

She held a hand out to shake on it and I complied.

Maya and I promised to continue our conversation later. I strolled into Talbot's tattoo shop, and he was arguing with Garret, while Diya was talking with Tim and Scottie.

"Sir, we have to put the banners up. It's a promo banner."

"I don't care what it is. I said you could use my place of business; I didn't say you could change everything and make it into the White House," Talbot fumed, pointing at the flyers and pencils with my campaign slogan on them: "We're better together—Ethan West for Governor."

I stood to the side, watching as Garret turned red. "Sir…"

"Stop calling me 'sir.' I'm not some seventy-year-old man. I'm probably just a year or two older than you," Talbot grumbled.

"Talbot, what is going on?" Diya interrupted.

"This guy is turning my business into the oval office. Ethan's grinning like something's funny."

Diya sighed, pulling him away.

"Garret, we can do without the banner. I think people will know what's happening," I emphasized, patting him on the shoulder.

"Yes, sir," Garret answered, walking off to finish prepping.

Genesis sauntered inside and Scottie ran into his arms, kissing him on the cheek. He embraced her tightly, whispering in her ear. Whatever it was caused a longing in each of their eyes. Something I was starting to want for myself more and more.

"Ethan, the place looks great," Genesis said, breaking me out of a trance.

"Because of your wife, Talbot, and Diya. Did you see the column response that Scottie oversaw?"

"I tell her all the time she could run her own paper and help people, because she gives the best advice, and then I remember that would have her away from me for long periods of time," Genesis said.

She raised her eyes to find him watching her.

"Don't let him fool you," Scottie teased.

"Where's Talbot?" Genesis asked.

"Right here," Talbot responded, walking over with Diya under his arms. He seemed much calmer and happy now.

"The place looks great, Talbot. Are you seeing more clients at this new location?" Genesis said, holding Scottie's hand.

"The first shop is still my primary spot, where my high-profile clientele go. I let Diya run this one more, since we hired a lot of new tattoo artists," Talbot said, right as Gage and Nina stepped inside, fussing.

"This is all your fault. I told you to pull out," Nina harshly grimaced in frustration.

"Baby doll, that will never happen. I can't help that you seduced me," Gage joked.

Nina balled up her fists, ready to attack.

"What is the commotion about, you two? Ethan is about to have fifty guests any minute and the last thing he needs is celebrity baseball player Gage and his wife on the front-page news." Scottie scowled.

"I'm pregnant," Nina mumbled.

"What?" Diya questioned.

"He got me pregnant again!" Nina said, upset, before she stomped off to the back.

"Oh..." Scottie and Diya said at the same time. Glaring at Gage, they shook their heads in disappointment.

Shrugging, Gage seemed very pleased with himself.

Scottie and Diya followed Nina to get her to calm down.

"This makes number four, right?" Genesis queried.

Gage rubbed his hands together, showing signs of determination.

"I told her I was going for a baseball team and she didn't believe me. She's mostly worried we'll have another set of twins."

"You're not?" I asked.

"I'm thinking this is my last year of playing, so retirement is near, and Tailynn is getting older. I want to be around more as she grows into a young lady. Nina works from home more and I can admit I miss my family when I travel to away games," Gage confessed.

"Talbot has the best relationship because Diya works with him," I hinted.

Genesis hiked his brows. "Gage will figure it out, but the most important thing is making sure she feels supported."

There was a loud crash, and all eyes turned to Garret. A tip jar for donations to Nina's community had broken and scattered on the floor. Talbot retained his affability, but there was a distinct hardening of his eyes.

"Ethan, you owe me after this," Talbot warned, walking off in the direction of Garret and Tim.

"Gage, how did you deal with the media surrounding your relationship with Nina in the beginning?" I wondered.

"The hurdle was rough at first, especially with my background with dating. Nina was tough and seeing how the blogs wanted to make it seem like she was in it for the money after we got married didn't help. I was glad it didn't cause any stress on her once the babies came. You and Maya good?"

"Still figuring things out."

Scottie came over and tapped Gage on the shoulder, gesturing for him to follow her to the back with Nina. If she wanted me to kick Gage's ass for making her cry, then I would, but then she'd be pissed that we weren't talking after just becoming friends again.

"I can't stay long; I have a meeting to get to myself. I wanted to let you know my private investigator found out

Hannah got locked up for trespassing after you called the psych ward. Her parents had her released a day later, and she showed up at West Bank. Jeffrey said she was meeting with Cody," Genesis said.

"I was prepared for this."

"If I were you, I would fire him. You've come too far to have your campaign tainted with any more drama. Even the smallest inclination that your executive is working with your ex-girlfriend will give the media a field day."

"You're right. After we finish hosting this event, I'll focus on handling the situation at the office." We shook hands and agreed to continue the conversation when the rally was over.

Scottie picked up the microphone to make an announcement.

"Thank you all for coming today. Talbot, I know the look of the shop is not what you're used to, and I promise to have Ethan pay for any damage that is caused," she joked, and everyone laughed as Talbot pointed at me.

"Ethan invited you all here to say thank you for your continued support. He approached me about coming on to help get him elected and at first, I was a little nervous because we all know how the typical cocky, business suit wearing man from Wall Street tends to be. Honestly, Ethan is a great friend of mine and my husband. Gage has endorsed his campaign and even allowed ads to run. Normally he stays out of the political ring. The latest numbers show him in the lead as we go into the first debate. With a warm welcome please clap and shout for the one and only, Ethan West!" Scottie said, passing me the mic.

"Scottie, I don't know how I can top that speech. Genesis, is she always like this?"

He yelled out. "Yes!"

The crowd cheered and laughed.

"That's good to know. As Scottie stated, I want to personally thank you all for coming today and supporting me on this journey. I see my parents in the back, and my assistant, Carol. A lot of familiar faces. Many of you know, I'm very tough in business; some can even say 'bossy in general.' I know what I want, and how it needs to get done. Running for governor is another way for me to give back to New York, the city I was born and raised in. This won't be an easy road, as we've all seen over the past few weeks from the lies in the papers and on the blogs. But you've stayed on with your support, and I promise not to let you down."

The crowd started chanting my name, whistling, and clapping as I stood there.

* * *

I introduced my parents to Tim and Garret, mixing and mingling with the crowd as drinks were passed around. I signed a few autographs, took pictures, and hung out with friends before the chaos really started.

Chapter 18

Maya

One month later

The first debate was today and I stood off to the side with Larry, waiting for Ethan to take the stage with the other candidate. It was down to him and Robert Lanton, another Independent candidate that seemed to play dirty politics. Every other day his face was on an ad about Ethan as some stuck-up rich businessman that was only doing this for money.

Speak of the devil, I thought to myself.

Robert snaked his way over and shook Ethan's hand with a fake smile on his face.

"Get a shot of this, Larry."

"On it."

"Douglas wants to do a one-on-one comment with Ethan either before or after. So, make sure you have enough footage on you."

Focusing on the two men, Larry nodded in answer.

Out of the corner of my eye, I saw Tim come up to Ethan letting him know it was time to get on stage.

I followed to the front of the stage, off to the side with

the other reporters as the lights flashed that it was time to be quiet.

"Ladies and gentlemen, we are here today to hear from both candidates. I ask you all to please not clap or boo. No matter the answer, we need to get through everything to make sure each candidate has enough time. Thank you," Reporter Wendy Simmons of FBX News said.

Ethan and Robert both introduced themselves and the first question was asked.

"Mr. West, I have to ask because we've all seen it in the media over the past few months, your relationship status; single, married, or dating?" Wendy questioned.

"I like to keep my private life private, Wendy. The people of New York want to hear about when the subway will stop breaking down, and if they'll have food on the table the next day," Ethan stated confidently, winking at the camera.

"For a follow up question, what can you tell us about your company, West Bank Investments? I hear there's a little bit of corporate takeover and fighting between the VP and CEO? I know the people of New York want to know if you couldn't handle running your own business, how will you manage a city?" Wendy directed back at him.

"Same thing I'd like to know," Robert snidely clipped.

"Any businessman will tell you that the transition from old guard to new takes time and making sure it's in the right hands when you have hundreds of people depending on you is delicate. I say this all the time, and I'll continue to not apologize for making money. This country was built on the promise of working hard and reaping the rewards. The decisions in my company have built it into what it is today as the largest banking system in the world. The dealings with my ex-employee and VP are being investigated," he stated.

The crowd started clapping and the security inside whispered for everyone to calm down. Deep down I wanted to run up there and kiss him.

* * *

After the debate ended, Ethan invited me to his home. I kicked off my heels grabbing a fork and plate to taste some of the soul food his housekeeper made. "How long have you worked for him?" I asked as she scooped up some mashed potatoes, mac and cheese, and meatloaf.

"Since he was a little baby. Drove me crazy never staying put, always talking numbers and now look at him running for governor," she lovingly spoke.

He was out of his suit jacket with no tie, sleeves rolled up, sitting next to me at the kitchen island stuffing his face and watching the feedback from reporters and commentators.

"She loved it," Ethan pushed, getting her riled up. I liked their relationship; she was more of a second mom to him.

"Boy, don't make me pop you." She held the wooden spoon up. "I'm going to bed."

"Night!" the both of us answered.

He grabbed my plate and motioned for me to follow him.

"You have to give me a tour of your place one day," I commented.

"I'll do that. Take a seat," Ethan demanded, putting our plates on the side table.

"I like how you decorated this room. Is this your man room or something? I see all of your plaques hanging up."

He grasped my legs moving them onto his lap.

"You rub feet? Don't let me find out you have a foot fetish," I teased.

"For the right person I can have whatever fetish that pleases her."

Changing the subject before I ended up naked on the couch, I said, "I got a lot of great footage tonight with you on stage. I saw your parents there cheering you on."

He ran a hand up from my ankle, to my thigh. "My mom was able to not embarrass me for once."

"The numbers coming in have you in the lead. Are you nervous if you really win?"

"Only thing that makes me nervous is you."

"Me?" I pointed at myself.

"You." He stopped rubbing my thigh and moved my legs off his lap. "I have a car waiting for you outside to take you home. We both have a long day tomorrow with the game and I need to take care of some things before the next debate."

I didn't know what happened to cause the shift in the conversation, but I wasn't waiting around to find out. Picking up my heels, purse, and jacket, I left not caring what he said.

...

"Come on Tailynn, you got this!" I screamed from the benches. Emery, Scottie, Diya, and I came to see Tailynn's game. Nina normally coached, but she was still taking some time off and her assistant was managing things in her absence. She was still hanging near the coach's dugout giving out orders. It was funny seeing Gage telling her to stand down, when he's the one normally yelling and trying to coach Tailynn from the benches.

"Good job, Celine, run, run!" Diya and I shouted at the same time, jumping up and clapping as she hit the ball.

"Is this first game the one that will determine if they go to the championship?" asked Scottie as she passed the bucket of popcorn.

"Yeah, and their five and nine streak in the league. I told her and Tailynn we'd take them for a spa day if they win," I replied.

"I can always use a spa day."

Diya held her hand up for the drink caddy. "You want something?" she asked.

"No, I cut back on soda, grab me a bottle of water please," I answered.

"Did Ethan tell you his first debate returns show him in the lead? We have two more and then people's final vote. I think I'm more nervous than him." Scottie reminded me of the one person I was avoiding.

"Good for him."

"What happened now?" Diya inquired.

"She's pissed at Ethan," Scottie said, taking the soda out of Diya's hand.

"No, I'm not. We're fine," I exclaimed.

Tailynn and Celine ran over to us. "Auntie Maya, can we come to your house for a movie and junk food please?" Tailynn begged.

"Sure, ask your parents if it's okay."

"We can make it a girls' night," Emery said.

"Let's meet at my place in thirty minutes with your

pajamas. I have this new avocado and lemon mask that's supposed to get rid of the wrinkles immediately," I boasted. I watched her run off to her parents to get permission and was unsurprised five minutes later when she quickly returned. I knew they wanted to dump the kids off on someone else for the evening.

"Okay, Daddy said that's fine and Mommy said I can ride with you. She's going to make sure the twins get settled and meet us at your house," Tailynn said, picking up her gym bag. Finishing off the last bit of popcorn, we all left together heading back to my place.

The girls started recording themselves on TikTok doing the latest dance moves and I joined in as we got closer to the car.

"Go, Maya! Go, Maya!" they shouted together.

Forty minutes later, we pulled into my garage and grabbed the bags of groceries, which was mostly junk food, for tonight.

"Girls, take the keys and open the door please," I told them.

Tailynn opened the door and dropped her bag on the kitchen floor then took off to turn on the TV.

"Tailynn, pick up your bag and go change. Just because you're at Maya's house doesn't mean you don't still need to follow the same rules. And don't make me have to repeat myself. Take Celine to the guest room so she can change," Nina reprimanded her.

Tailynn was at that age of thinking she knew everything and having a father that spoiled her rotten was not helping.

"Reminds me of Nicole," I said, dropping the bag on the counter before taking my purse and jacket off. Kicking off my shoes, I opened the freezer to put the ice cream away. Nina started to grab a bowl for the chips and tray for the candy.

"How are you feeling about the pregnancy since you announced everything at Talbot's event?" I questioned.

Before she could respond, Scottie and Diya came inside already wearing their pajamas.

"I got the wine!" Scottie said excitedly. She opened the drawer next to the sink and picked up the wine opener. Celine and Tailynn came into the kitchen and grabbed the chips and candy.

"At first, I was pissed, that man. Tailynn, can you and Celine go pick a movie out please?"

They skipped out of the kitchen happily.

"I love sex, but Gage is like a 7-Eleven; open all night. I can be wearing a onesie with my hair in rollers and he'll still want to jump my bones," Nina exaggerated, taking the mint chip ice cream out of the freezer and making a sundae.

"That's a good problem to have right? I mean, I'm not married, but you always want your husband to think you're sexy?" I asked.

"I can count on my hands before I got married, the amount of dates I went on. Do you remember the guy that took me on a date almost to a funeral? If getting seen as a sex symbol by your husband is a problem, then sign me up, because going backwards I can only imagine the dating life now," Scottie said.

"I agree with Maya and Emery. Nina, talk with him and tell him how you feel. The last thing we need you doing is running off like Scottie did without talking to Genesis," Diya said.

"I forgot about that. Gage would have all the airports

shut down before I even thought of stepping on a plane to California," Nina admitted.

"You helped me," Scottie said, rolling her eyes.

"The movie's starting!" Tailynn yelled from the living room.

"Here we come. I'm going to change quickly. Can you pay for the pizza when he gets here? I ordered ahead already," I stated, leaving out of the kitchen to go change into my pajamas.

A few minutes later I was back in the living room with the girls eating the pizza, wearing the avocado mask on their faces, and painting nails.

"What color is that, Emery? It looks yellowish or something," I wondered, sitting down on the couch taking a slice of pizza.

"A mixture of off white and yellow together. I had the nail shop create it for me," Emery said, blowing over Celine's nails to help them dry faster.

"Tailynn, are you going to help me put on my face mask?"

She nodded jumping up from the floor and grabbing the bowl of green mud off the counter with a spoon and towel.

"This is cold, Auntie," Tailynn reminded me.

"Gotcha. So, tell me, how is school going for you two? Any boys calling?"

Celine and Tailynn peered at each other and then shook their heads no. "I see girl code is already started with you two. Keeping secrets, huh?" I playfully joked.

"We can't say anything. At one point we acted like that when we were their age," Diya said.

Nina, Scottie, and I all spoke at the same time, "Yep."

"Hell, Nicole acts like that now at her age, so some people never grow out of it," Nina said.

"What do your parents think of her traveling as a DJ?" Diya said, taking the bowl of chips.

"What can they say other than make sure you have money to get home and don't call us if you get into trouble. Nicole is still finding herself and pushing my lifestyle on her wouldn't work," Nina preached.

"I feel you on the parents part. I got into it with my mom and she slapped me. It makes me appreciate the relationship you two have with Tailynn and Celine," I admitted.

"Hey, this ladies' night is getting too serious, turn on some Beyoncé and Tailynn can show us that dance they did earlier today." Scottie stood grabbing the remote off the table and turning the movie down and music up.

Celine was by her side explaining the first steps and Tailynn finished putting on the mask and went to show Nina the same moves. Seeing my friends as moms was weird because we've all come a long way from where we started and the growth and journey for each of our paths led us to this point in life finally being fulfilled.

Chapter 19

Ethan

"I want you out of my company now. You are no longer needed. I suggest you leave willingly before I have you thrown out."

"You're not in charge anymore. Ever since you went off to play God, I'm the one that has kept this ship going."

"Cody, you seem to think I give a damn what you think of me. I fucking built this with my own two hands. I'm looking at the evidence right here that you've been in cahoots with *Gloss Gossip Magazine* and my opponent, Robert Lanton, to discredit me. Here are the photos for everyone to see. Hannah can't save you, because she's being taken into custody as we speak for blackmail. Now if you want to join her, I can set that up for you?"

"Those photos are fake. You planted that on me to get me out of here because I wanted to bring in a mutual board to oversee things instead of your family member being CEO!" he yelled.

"Funny you say 'board,' because Genesis Maguire was the one that put the call in from *Gloss Gossip Magazine* and his contact told us that you've been sending them paperwork for the last two years of deals that my bank has done. On top of making Richard help you steal from me. What? You didn't think we'd notice the two million missing was traced back to you?" I asked.

He looked shocked at my admission.

"You're not fit to run a business or an office," Cody snapped.

"Why?"

"People like you make me sick. Handed a silver spoon in their mouth and think you can walk all over people."

"Don't push me," I grunted, pointing a finger in his face, ready to pound his smug face in.

"This isn't over. I can promise that. I have people in high places just like you, Ethan."

"Then you should know that we sent your information over to the police and IRS.

Seems the last ten years you've kept some things away from being disclosed. I'd think all those trips to Russia would need to be disclosed, seeing as how you've made over twenty million, and I know Ethan hasn't paid you that well over the past few years," Genesis gritted, opening the door for the police as they approached with cuffs in their hand.

"Take him," Genesis said.

"You think it's finished?" I questioned as they led a cuffed Cody out of the office.

"I'm not sure, Ethan, most of the time these things can bring up even more problems."

I grabbed my coat and followed behind Genesis.

"Are you meeting Scottie?" Genesis asked.

"I need to prepare her and Tim for what's about to come out."

"We can head to my place. She's home," Genesis said.

* * *

An hour later, we walked in his home with Celine and Scottie sitting down on the floor watching the latest *Spotlight with Maya* episode on Fashion.

"How are you two doing, and where's my son?"

"He's asleep, and don't you go waking him up," Scottie blasted.

Genesis grinned, kissing her on the lips.

"Hi, Ethan!" Celine said.

I reached over and gave Celine a hug, and she ran off to the kitchen.

"Why the gloomy face?" Scottie asked.

Leaning back on the couch, I sighed harshly. "I fired Cody. We found out he was working with Hannah and using Richard. They stole money from me and tried to ruin my name."

"Where is he now?" Scottie asked, picking up the toys off the floor and placing them in the toy bin next to the door. Genesis walked back out with Celine following behind, holding her phone up, talking to someone.

"The police took him into custody. As his senior advisor, you should get ahead of the story before the media tries to throw any dirt on the campaign," Genesis told her, taking a seat on the couch, pulling Scottie to sit on his lap.

"I'll contact Tim to see what he's heard. The good news is that the responses from the *Candidate Corner Column* are going well, and they're talking about wanting to do another one if you're interested after you become governor."

"Keyword here is if I become governor."

Scottie waved me off. "Don't stress about it now. I'm

going to start lunch, do you want to stay and eat with us?" Scottie asked, right as their son started crying.

"I got him," Genesis said, tapping her on the thigh to stand up, and she maneuvered over to the kitchen.

"Sure."

Celine waved into the phone, and I saw Tailynn with Maya in the background.

"Celine! Did you see the new *Sonic* movie trailer? Maya's taking me to see it today, you want to go?" Tailynn asked over the phone.

"I have to ask my parents," Celine said.

Thinking about Maya, I took my phone out of my pocket and texted her.

Me: *What are you wearing?*

Maya: *I'm wearing jeans and a shirt about to head to work.*

Me: *Dinner tonight?*

Maya: *Nope.*

Me: *Why not?*

Maya: *LOL! I've got a date.*

Me: *You don't date if I remember your exact words. You have gentlemen friends for pleasure only.*

Maya: *A date with my dad, silly. My sister and I go out with him, just us girls.*

Me: *Afterwards, you should come over.*

Maya: *So, you're not playing games anymore? Your lack of communication is trying my patience, Sir.*

Her using Sir caused a rumble in my chest.

Me: *Sorry. Work is getting hectic, but this week I'll make more time.*

Maya: *When you find the time, then call me. No sooner and no bullshit.*

Genesis offered me a beer while holding his son.

"Here you go." A part of me wondered what it would be like to have a child of my own, and then that idea went out the window with the way my life was set up.

"How is fatherhood treating you?"

The baby fussed in his arms. "The best feeling in the world. I want more, so I will see what Mommy says."

"Mommy says, she's waiting until little guy here gets older," Scottie said, passing Celine a snack of fruit and sandwich until dinner was ready.

I stayed over, talking and conversing with Scottie about the next debate, and Tim never showed as he was stuck with another client in Boston. Later that night, I went home alone and focused on my following campaign speech.

"You're coming in early at ten o'clock; something must be on your mind," Athena stated.

"What are you still doing up? You usually are in bed watching your Real Housewife shows," I retorted.

She waved me off, pouring a cup of hot chocolate.

"I couldn't sleep, and tonight's a rerun. Where are you coming from?"

"Scottie and Genesis's."

"Did you eat already? I can warm you up some food."

"I did."

"The long face is telling me you fucked up, and you don't know how to fix it."

Running a hand across my face, I said, "After Hannah, I'm still on the border about making things serious with Maya. As we get closer, I seem to pull back a little each time. Then on top of that, I know she's not the type to fall in love, and what if a few years from now, I want kids and she doesn't?"

"You're making a lot of assumptions for something

that hasn't happened yet. Talk to her and see where her head is at. We both know that Hannah was a looney tune and a gold digger from the beginning. Not everyone is like that."

I chuckled at her comment as she walked off to her bedroom. *Once the election is over, we can discuss if we want to continue a relationship,* I thought to myself.

Chapter 20

Maya

"This is *Spotlight with Maya Armstrong*. Remember, the tea never spills without my stamp of approval. See you next time," I said excitedly, closing out the show as the camera crew signaled that the red light was off, and we were not live anymore.

Keisha followed behind me toward the dressing room and makeup station.

"Good episode, Maya. The shows with Ethan are going good with you following the campaign," Keisha said, using the makeup wipes to clean my face.

"Thanks, Keisha, I think it helps that he has close friends of mine on the campaign to help get me into rooms that I normally wouldn't be in as a talk show host," I answered.

"How is it going with him and the debates?"

"Good. He won the last two debates and has a third and final one this week before the election. Have you decided on who you're voting for?" I inquired.

"Your man, of course."

I tapped her on the arm with the brush for being loud. "No one knows we're seeing each other, and I want to keep it that way, please."

"Honey, what's the point of dating a billionaire if you can't tell anybody? Plus, he's going to be the governor. I would shout that from the rooftop if it were me."

"Good it's not you then."

"Rude much," Keisha replied snarkily.

"Sorry, the truth is I have to deal with not only him, but I haven't spoken to my mom in almost two months, and I might have an opportunity out of state, so things are going at a fast pace for me now," I told her.

"What? Are you serious? Tell me!"

"Fine, the footage of my work on Ethan's campaign has interested a lot of people in California and Seattle to do the morning talk show slot with either *Good Morning Seattle* or possibly have my own mainstream talk show, and then there's a broadcasting deal in California and I need to decide soon about going out to interview. Mostly for testing, but from what they've said, I'm the number one pick."

"Wow!"

"I know."

"If you did go, what would happen with you and Ethan?"

"That's the question I've asked myself for the past few weeks. Either he's working late, or I'm working late here and on my blog. Plus, Kasey is staying with me now until she gets another place."

"Your mom?"

"She's my mother. Stubborn and selfish like me, I guess. Not ready to apologize first."

"Listen to me, you're nothing like your mother. Get that out of your head right now, and whatever happens with you and Ethan is meant to be. Focus on yourself and what your dreams are. I remember you've always wanted this to happen, and it's finally coming true."

"Thanks, Keisha, I'm about to head out for lunch with the girls, do you want to come?" I grabbed my purse and keys to head out for the day. We didn't have a meeting since Douglas was out sick today, and I had more free time to prepare for the final debate and nomination.

"I have another show I have to do makeup and hair on. Let the girls know I said hello," Keisha said. She grabbed her makeup kit and bag strolling over to the next sound-stage around the corner of a music competition show.

Sliding into my car, I dropped my bag and purse on the seat and put the key in the ignition, backing up and driving off the lot. Turning at the light after showing my ID badge, my phone rang, and I checked as the light turned red.

Kasey: *Where are you?*

Me: *Heading to meet Diya and Nina for lunch.*

Kasey: *You finished filming for the day?*

Me: *Yes, you want to join us?*

Kasey: *Yeah, I'm done at the library.*

Me: *Okay, heading to Jane's.*

The light turned green, and I took off onto the expressway to get there faster. New York traffic was heavy all day long, so it didn't matter if I was planning to meet at a certain time or not, more than likely I would be late.

Thirty minutes later, I arrived at Jane's, and the girls

were sitting outside. Checking my makeup and hair, I stepped out of the car and headed to the table, observing that they sat up front to be noticed.

"She finally made it, how was work?" Nina questioned.

Placing my purse on the arm of the chair, I rolled my sleeves up and took a sip of the water.

"It was good, and I did two shows today, so they'll last me for two weeks. I can have extra footage with me on the campaign stops for the final debate. How are things with you and Gage? I see your little pooch showing."

I rubbed across her little belly.

"Fine, the team is playing well and might be headed to the playoffs again," Nina explained.

"What about you, Diya? How's the shop after Ethan's little event session? Is Talbot speaking to him yet?" I cackled at her facial expression. Talbot was furious because Garret invited a band to play, and neither Talbot nor Ethan knew about it, and the entire time they stayed outside playing old school music. The next day, Talbot called and said if he weren't friends with Ethan, he would have banned Garret from ever stepping foot in his shop.

"Garrett meant well, but we all know Talbot does not play about his shop, and Garrett was going way overboard to get some publicity," Diya reminded.

The news these past few weeks had had a steady rotation of Ethan and his company in the media about a VP getting arrested and embezzling money and funneling it to Russia. Also, he was working with Hannah, Ethan's ex, to make him look bad. The poll numbers had gone up and down, but he still won the last few debates against Robert.

"Scottie called me laughing so hard after she took a

photo of the band outside wearing Ethan's shirts with his slogan."

"Did you talk to Ethan?"

"Not yet. Our schedules are just all over the place," I responded.

The server came over right as Kasey walked up. She took a seat opposite me at the four-seat table, and the server passed us both a menu.

Taking a chip and some salsa, I already knew what I wanted and didn't need to read over anything.

"Hi, ladies, I'm Melody. I have their orders. Did you need a few minutes?"

"I'm ready. Can I get the miso soup and salad, please? More chips and salsa with an iced tea, sweetened," I answered.

"You can bring me the same thing as her," Kasey commented, giving her menu back.

"Kasey, I'm loving the hair, what made you cut it?" Nina queried.

"Life," Kasey said.

"What's wrong?"

She sighed, peering around the room.

"I met a guy, and I don't think Mommy will like him," she answered.

"Forget her," I said sarcastically.

"Maya, don't say that. What's the problem with her now?" Diya scolded.

"She's determined to ruin my life because Maya doesn't come around anymore, so I'm left with getting the annoying pressure of being the perfect daughter," Kasey spat, rolling her eyes.

"Life is too short to please everybody, but yourself," I challenged.

"One of those times where I can agree with your sister. Normally she's bat shit crazy and selfish, but I see her letting her shell come down and know that's because of Ethan. Listen to your sister, Kasey, and follow your heart. I was lucky with Gage; my parents didn't care who I dated or married, more so if he treated me good and Gage does. The parents won't always be there, so you need to not let her opinions get into your head." Nina spoke truth to power with that last statement.

"Where's Scottie?" Kasey questioned.

"With Ethan. I called her to see if she wanted to join us, and they were finishing up some interview with a celebrity talk show or something," Diya stated.

"Are you two still good?" Nina asked, nudging me in the shoulder.

"I guess. I haven't told him about the possible talk show interviews I have coming up."

Kasey choked on her lemonade as I reached over to pat her on the back.

"You have interviews for where?"

"Seattle and California!" I blurted out.

"Maya! Oh my god! You're leaving me." Kasey pouted like a little kid.

We all giggled at her humped over posture with her hand covering her face.

"Kasey, you need to calm down. I haven't gotten the job yet, and it's only an interview. Technically I have it if I want the job. It's just a matter of figuring out which one."

"Do Mommy and Daddy know?"

"Dad knows," I answered.

Melody brought our food out, and we started to eat and continue the conversation.

"He's okay with you leaving?" Diya inquired.

Shrugging my shoulders in a show of indifference, I replied, "I mean he's not gung-ho about it, but I'm a grown woman, and it's an opportunity for me to branch out to a wider market."

"Yeah, until Ethan goes to put that *D* in you and change your mind," Kasey insisted.

Waving her off, we continued laughing at her getting emotional about me possibly leaving. The way Ethan was set up, he'd probably be grateful I was going so he could move on to his next bedmate.

Chapter 21

Ethan & Maya

Maya

The sun was bright and shining outside while we sat inside his campaign office having lunch. I suggested we go somewhere private, but he insisted on showing the world he had nothing to hide amid the hustle and bustle of the phones ringing nonstop and interns and volunteers coming inside. Ethan had ordered lunch for the both of us.

"What do you think your parents feel about the media attention with the scandal finally turning tides?"

"I explained to them that Cody was fucking things up behind my back, and Hannah was helping him. My father didn't care, my mother was worried I would go to jail, and I told her things are fine. Genesis helped get all the documents that Cody had forged my name or the accounting numbers on."

"Huh."

"What's on your mind, Maya? I can tell you're a little standoffish right now," Ethan stated, pushing a piece of hair behind my ear.

"Nothing. Ready for the final debate so I can see you walk up on the stage and give a speech about your plans as the new governor," I said, putting the fork down.

"Am I going to see you later tonight?"

"Are you admitting that you missed me over the past few weeks?" I asked, crossing my legs, and sitting back against the couch in his office.

"I miss that mouth of yours every day," he teased, running his thumb over my bottom lip.

I leaned over and kissed him as he wrapped his arms around my waist, rubbing my ass in the black tights I wore with a long white dress shirt.

I moaned against his lips as he smacked my ass.

"Don't start anything. You know I can't finish with a building full of people here," he groaned, squeezing my ass again.

"Touché, sir."

"Do you realize when you call me Mr. West or Sir, that it causes my dick to get even harder?" he confessed.

"Which means the moment you see me, you're already hard at the first sight of me, and then when I do this," I kissed him again, circling my tongue in his mouth, reaching my hand down, rubbing against his ample girth, "you get even harder."

* * *

"Stop playing with me."

"I like when you get all flustered and turn red, you wear your emotions on your face."

"So, then you know if you keep rubbing what'll happen, right?" I challenged.

"I do, and it's not happening here."

"I want you to meet my parents at the next debate," I muttered, holding her in place.

"As your friend, girlfriend, or media reporter?" she asked, pulling away from me and sitting up.

Before I could answer there was a knock at the door and Scottie and Tim walked in.

"Hello you two, we need to steal him for a little while. Maya, do you mind?" Scottie asked.

That interruption caused Maya to close back off, and I reached for her hand. She jerked back, grabbing her purse and keys to leave.

"Is everything all right in here?" Scottie raised her left eyebrow at me.

I held my hand up in surrender.

"Maya, let me walk you out," I exclaimed.

"No, finish your work. I'll see you tomorrow at the debate."

I sighed in frustration and watched as she swayed out of my office with an attitude. Getting involved with a woman seriously was rough. I didn't want our relationship to hinder our goals or make me vulnerable again. I didn't want to end up hurt. That's not how I wanted to enter my office as governor.

"Did you do something to my friend?" Scottie pointed a pen in my face, her right hand on her hip.

"Scottie, calm down. We have work to do, and his personal life is off-limits for discussion. It's better he keeps things under wraps with her anyway," Tim said.

He must not have ever met Scottie Maguire before because the way she turned around fast like lighting, was hilarious.

Tim jumped back when she poked him in the chest.

"Tim, realize one thing; I protect my family and

friends. I don't care whose campaign I'm on. This means nothing to me if my friend ends up hurt over it. Do I make myself clear?" Scottie emphasized.

"Yes. Crystal...clear," he stuttered.

"Good. Now, Ethan, tell me what happened with Maya and don't leave anything out because the last time we talked, you wanted to invite her to the nomination party and to meet your parents." Scottie sat on the edge of my desk.

"What about the poll numbers?" Tim demanded.

"They're fine for right now, we need to discuss more important things like why my best friend is upset with your candidate."

"*My* candidate!" Tim and I shouted at the same time.

"Yep, I told you at any time I would stop working with you if I felt someone I loved was harmed with you running for governor."

"Scottie, I promise it's not that serious. At the same time, I'm not discussing my personal life with you."

"Told you," Tim jested.

Scottie rolled her hips and stood up from the edge of the desk, crossing her arms over her chest.

"Okay."

"Okay, that's all you have to say to him?" Tim questioned, offended she didn't snap on me like she did with him. I chuckled at his facial expression.

"He gets one pass with me. After that, no more, so let's get down to business," Scottie said, opening the file with the poll numbers and the notes for the final debate.

"Things are looking good in your favor now that Cody is pleading guilty and not fighting against Hannah's admission of guilt. Richard ran off to Cuba, so we can't get him caught up on any charges. We need to focus on how you'll improve education because Robert will hit you below the belt about your company and the charges against your VP," Scottie stated, passing the piece of paper with Cody's and Hannah's mugshots from the *New York Business* newspaper. They posted all the latest in the business and finance world. A few months back, they posted Genesis's charity event and the endorsement of my race for Governor and a week later, plastered about the shit Hannah was doing behind the scenes with a fake video, and nude photos.

"I agree with her about Robert, and he's going to try and rip you apart as out of touch and working with the swamp. You need to hammer it down about the education crisis and how you'll raise the minimum wage for families in New York."

"Okay, how many reporters are we looking at for the nomination night? I want to give Maya the exclusive interview if I win."

"That can be arranged," Scottie said, writing a list. I rented out the Waldorf for campaign night with my supporters to watch the results, and the minute we got the numbers back, we'd party whether or not the results were in our favor.

"Shouldn't you interview with the major news stations first? I like Maya, but we need to get the message across, you're not the flashy celebrity candidate from her show, or the segments she's posted. The people want a leader they can trust and believe in, and if you're seen with Hollywood type of people, they'll think you're not serious about the needs of the people," Tim explained.

"He might have a point, Ethan."

"You agree with Tim?" I asked, shocked because they usually were opposites in how to go about things.

"This one time, if we have you walking off stage and interviewing her first and all the flashes go off, it could seem a little Hollywood, because you have her on the debates with you every time and on the bus getting one-on-one close up interviews. We need to show the people you can take questions from any outlet, even ones that don't agree with your policies."

Scottie made a good point, and I hoped Maya would understand.

"Arrange it then, and let Maya know I will still interview with her, and she should be sitting in my friends and family section."

They both nodded in agreement, and we went over the food and my attire for the night, deciding on a dark black suit with an American flag pin, subtle but not over the top.

"Who's doing the debate questions?"

"Wendy again," Tim fussed.

"You don't like her?" Scottie wondered.

Tim blew out a breath of frustration.

"The woman is looking for her fifteen minutes of fame and riding on the coattails of all the shit that Hannah pulled, trying to do a gotcha moment with Ethan. I can't stand a reporter that shows off their biases at face value just because he has money. She thinks we're buying the election, and that couldn't be further from the truth," Tim exclaimed.

"That's the media, though. We have to suck it up and continue to keep the message to the people and at the end of the day, they vote. As long as Ethan gives more than he takes out of the process and works those phone lines so people can build trust with him, we can win," Scottie preached.

"Damn, would you be my Lt. Governor?" I asked, trying to boost her ego.

She waved me off, laughing.

"Seriously, Scottie, because of you, I'm able to get this far. I owe you and Genesis big time."

"I'll hold you to that."

Chapter 22

Ethan

ne week later

The final debate. After months of campaigning and working long nights, I was finally on the stage ready to answer the ultimate questions and find out if New York would believe in my message.

"You ready, Ethan?" Tim asked, holding the note cards as I gulped water. Everyone was here tonight to cheer me on. My parents and friends, as well as a few employees from the bank. We hadn't dealt with any significant fallout as the campaign drew near, and I was thankful. I called Maya that night she left my office, and we talked on the phone about going out on a date once the election was over, and clearing the air about what we wanted out of this situation we found ourselves in. I stood with my hands in my pockets, listening to Tim run down every possible scenario he could come up with from Robert.

"Remember, he's going to go for the big government takeover ideas, and how we need to let people figure things out on their own. Focus on how you've been to the neighbors and talked with the kids and teachers, the school boards, and families on what's not working in the low-income areas."

"Can we please have all the candidates on stage?" the announcer called.

"There's my cue," I said.

The announcer called our names, and we each walked out and shook hands. I stepped over to my side of the stage with my nameplate on the front board. I took another sip of water and caught the high beam light next to Maya and my family.

I waved as they continued introductions.

"Gentlemen, we are here for the final debate, and I want to remind you to please keep your answers concise. Each person will get a chance for a rebuttal and answer. Then a closing statement. Audience, once again, please refrain from cheering or booing. We want to respect each person on the stage and give them time to answer questions," Wendy said, starting the clock.

"Thank you, Wendy," Robert and I said at the same time.

"The first question goes to Mr. Lanton. What do you feel about the current infrastructure in New York, and how would you go about improving things?"

He cleared his throat, loosening his tie a little. I could see the sweat beads across his forehead. "Good question, Wendy. I think we have a great infrastructure that can be improved with subsidies and working with the local businesses to give out loans to help rebuild the foundation we already have," Robert said.

"I disagree with giving more billions to these large corporations," I countered.

"That's because you're more interested in laying off more workers and leaving the unions behind," Robert spat.

"Gentlemen, please keep your answers directed toward me. Mr. West, same question."

"We shouldn't continue to reward bad behavior. Some of these companies charge the city millions and billions of dollars, and the work is shoddy. We have to be realistic with ourselves, and I do agree with Robert on the foundation. It's terrible, and we need to research because some of the pipes in New York are more than a hundred years old. Putting a band-aid on it won't help," I said.

"Mr. West, recently your ex-VP was arrested along with Hannah, your ex-girlfriend. Are we to understand they embezzled or tried to embezzle money out of you? I know as New Yorkers go into the polls, they want to know they can trust you have a team in place that's working for them and not to steal from our pockets," Wendy demanded.

"I can assure you, Wendy, the people of New York would have the best team behind me. I can say that loyalty is something I believe in, and that was broken. Going forward, each person that's hired under my leadership has been vetted or will be vetted once I become governor," I taunted Robert.

The crowd cheered and clapped at my statement.

"Robert, healthcare in New York, what are your plans?"

"We should put trust in the private sector and work with the insurance companies to lower prices as we work on lowering the taxes to open it up for more people to put onto insurance plans," Robert exclaimed.

"Free money to insurance corporations?" I grunted, annoyed with his answer. He was supposed to be an Independent like me and was now coming across more corporate-funded.

* * *

An hour later, the crowd went wild after we gave our last speech of the debate. I stood on the platform, talking with the media and letting them know how I felt about my overall performance and where I saw myself going in the future if I don't make it as the governor of New York.

"Some people are calling you the next Lincoln mixed with Obama. What do you have to say about that?" CVN asked, waiting for my answer.

"I think I've taken some things from all the great leaders I've studied, but I'm running as Ethan West and no copycat when I get into office."

"What do you think about your chances after tonight?" the AVB News reporter asked.

"I think I have a great chance, and I hope that New Yorkers understand what's at stake."

Shaking hands with other supporters and media outlets, I stood off to the side, taking pictures.

"Congrats Ethan! You nailed it, and you deserve to win," Diya said.

I hugged everyone as Maya walked over with my parents behind her.

"I think Diya's right, you nailed it tonight, and I could see Scottie prepping you a little with those answers," Maya joked.

"Aren't you Maya Armstrong of FBX?" the AVB reporter interrupted.

"I am, and tonight's about this guy," she responded.

Extending my hand, I took her to stand beside me as the flashes went off.

"Honey, you were wonderful up there. I think you got it in the bag," my mother said.

"Thank you. Maya, I want you to meet my parents, Lucy and Henry West."

Maya reached out to give them both a handshake.

"Ethan, the numbers are rolling in, and you're in the lead!" Scottie excitedly embraced Tim and me.

Genesis gently pulled her away from Tim and I, and we all laughed. I couldn't complain; I was the same way with Maya.

"We need to celebrate," I told them.

"The kids have school in the morning," Genesis reminded us.

"You're right. Have a drink for me, and I'll keep you updated over the next few days," Scottie commented.

"Saturday, we meet at the Waldorf, do we need anything else?" I asked, rubbing Maya's back as most of the crowd left out.

"Nope, we hired everyone and have the media lined up along with your speech if you win or lose."

"Thanks, Scottie," I said.

She hugged Maya and my parents again and walked out with Genesis.

"You coming home with me?" I whispered in my Maya's ear.

She innocently nodded.

Chapter 23

Maya

Once I left Ethan's place the other night, we'd talked and hammered our issues out. Meeting his parents was crazy because they seemed polar opposites of him. I already knew his cousin that was ruining him, and his live-in housekeeper.

Today, I was sitting in a meeting with Douglas and the head executives of Seattle's *Good Morning Seattle*.

"This would be a two-year deal for her?" Douglas inquired. He was trying to attach himself to the opportunity to go with me, and I didn't want any loose ends if I chose to further my career out of New York.

"Yes, and Maya has the hiring and firing control of her team. She would get an executive producer and co-creator credit on any shows she brings to us with a first-look deal," said Tomas, the head executive in charge of content.

"What if I wanted longer? Is there an opportunity to extend the contract?" I negotiated.

"We can discuss those terms, but the pay would stay the same because of your EP and co-creator with the option to extend depending on your numbers. You've been in the business for a while, you understand," Tomas stated.

"Everything looks good to me. Thank you, Tomas, we do need to talk with the California station, and we can have Maya call you later today with an answer," Douglas said, shaking his hand, escorting him to the door.

"Wow!" I exclaimed once we were alone.

"Sweet deal, Maya."

"Too sweet."

"You'll never get everything you want, but the power to make the major decisions is laid at your feet," Douglas informed me.

"I know, and I like the deal, but leaving my family for two years would be tough."

"What about us?" Douglas asked, grasping my hand.

I pulled my hand back. "Ummm, there is no us, Douglas."

"Maya, we've been seeing each other for months."

"Douglas, you ate my pussy a few times, and it wasn't even good. I faked it to hurry you up," I grumbled.

"You're lying!" he yelled, slamming his hand on the table, and I jumped.

"Lower your voice. I told you from the beginning I wasn't interested in a relationship, and besides, we haven't been intimate for almost six months or more. Stop acting like a baby and get out of your feelings," I demanded, standing up and walking out of the conference room and back to my office.

Arguing with him was the last thing on my mind today, and I would not baby him into thinking we would be anything more than co-workers.

I walked back into my office and almost passed out at

the funky smell of parmesan cheese. Attempting to not throw up on myself, I ran back out of the room and to the bathroom bursting through the door and pushing my way through the women screaming.

I barfed in the first stall that was open and felt someone pull my hair up out of my face.

"Are you okay, Maya?" Keisha asked, rubbing my back. I continued gagging and nodding my head. I was fine.

"Looks like someone may have interrupted her career plans with a baby," Tonya spat, taunting me.

I flushed the toilet and turned toward her with red hot eyes.

"Keep walking, Tonya, we don't need your input," Keisha said, helping me to stand.

She rolled her eyes and walked to the sink, and washed her hands, eyeing me.

"Is it Douglas's?" Tonya questioned, turning the water off.

"See now you're just asking for an ass whopping." Keisha pointed at the door for her to leave.

"He still won't love you, whoever the baby daddy is, and I do mean that loosely, we know you get around."

"You're mad. Douglas doesn't want you, Tonya," Keisha antagonized.

She finally left, and Keshia comforted me with a hug. I silently cried at the idea of me being pregnant and not wanting to decide if I should tell Ethan or not.

"Take the rest of the day off, and I'll go get you a test."

Forty minutes later, I was sitting in my bedroom next to Keisha, waiting for the timer to go off thinking about all the plans I put in place for my career and what pregnancy would mean.

"Don't overthink things, Maya, you can't make any decisions like this."

"I know." I sighed, right as my door opened, and my girls came inside.

"Don't look shocked. We've all been there, and Keisha called us when she bought the test. We told her we'd come right over," Nina explained.

Emery and Diya sat next to me on the floor. Nina's little pudge grew overnight as she looked three months pregnant now.

"Keisha, thanks for calling. I know Maya would have tried to handle this on her own without telling us a thing," Nina said, grabbing the throw blanket further up the bed.

"Last time you cleaned your room?" Diya stated.

"I have no clue. Work and hanging with Ethan has caused me to slack in some parts of my life," I answered right when the timer went off.

We all looked at each other, waiting to see what I would do.

"I'm going," I said.

Standing up, I walked into my oasis bathroom that would probably turn into a kid's playroom if I were pregnant and would never bring me solace and peace again.

Picking up the pregnancy stick, it had two blue lines lightly faded. I felt a presence behind me, and I turned around. Scottie and Nina grabbed the stick with a napkin, and their mouths dropped wide open when they saw the results.

"Are we happy or sad?" Nina spoke.

"I guess you'll have to add me to Mommy and Me classes in a few months." I groaned, falling back on the edge of the counter, rubbing my temples.

"What does it say!" Keisha shouted.

"Time to plan a shower!" Emery yelled back.
I need new friends, I thought to myself.

Chapter 24

Ethan

Saturday

The afternoon of the nomination results, I was at Maya's parents' house to talk with them. She was meeting me at the event, and I wanted to speak with them about both dating and how they'd have more security around them now that she was going to be in the public eye as my girlfriend.

Girlfriend.

Her father opened the door wearing a black double-breasted suit. His wife yelled from behind him.

"Who is it, Michael?"

"That boy Maya is dating," he answered.

I was shocked by his response.

I reached a hand out to shake his, and he motioned for me to enter.

"Thank you both for meeting me."

"Anytime, young man."

"Tonight's the night, right? I saw you on the TV voting earlier today," her mother, Hazel, asked.

"Yes, ma'am."

"We went and voted, and I told Maya to let you know we had all of our friends vote for you as well."

"I appreciate the vote of confidence," I responded.

"Maya's not here. We haven't, or I haven't seen her in a few months."

I remembered the discussion I had with Maya about the fight she had with her mother a few months back. It was to the point that her mother slapped her across the cheek. I understood why she was keeping her distance.

"I know, she told me about that."

"Lately, I've been getting some help because I know my husband is tired of the fighting between his girls and wife. I owe my family a large thank you for putting up with me for all these years," Hazel murmured.

"You should come to her birthday party I'm throwing for her. I came because I wanted to get your permission to ask for your daughter's hand in marriage."

"You are serious about her?" Michael questioned.

"Yes, sir, I am."

He smiled and extended a hand to me and hugged me with a pat on the back. "Take care of my baby girl," he stated.

"I will, sir, and I'll see you both tonight. The car will be here in about two hours."

Heading toward my car, I went back home to get dressed for tonight.

I finished getting dressed, and I checked myself out in the mirror. Grabbing my keys, I waited for Athena to get ready.

"How much longer is she going to need?" I asked the hairstylist and makeup artist.

"Almost ready, sir."

"Hush, Ethan, you can't rush perfection."

"You're already perfect to me; this was added to you for no reason." I buttered her up.

"You'll tell me anything to hurry me up."

We all burst out in laughter.

The driver knocked on the door and I went to greet him.

"Five minutes, ladies!" I shouted. I opened the door and let him know I'd be out soon.

...

As we got into the car, we swung by to pick up my parents and headed to the hotel. I checked my phone to text Maya. She still hadn't replied.

"Stop worrying; she'll be there," Athena said.

"I'm not worried."

Deep down, I was terrified. It wasn't just the election; I was putting my heart on the line.

Me: *I can't wait to see you tonight.*

A few minutes later, the bubbles came up that she read my message.

Maya: *I'm here with the girls now, and my parents just walked inside.*

Me: *Save me a kiss.*

Maya: *I'll think about it, Mr. West.*

Me: *Don't be bad over this phone with me sitting next to my parents.*

Maya: *I'll think about it, sir.*

I mumbled under my breath I was going to spank her after the results were announced because she was playing with my emotions.

We arrived at the hotel with paparazzi already outside, and news stations lined up. I helped my mother and Athena out of the car, and we all walked inside. I saw Scottie and Tim standing at the door, and they waved me over, taking my parents' coats.

"You look nervous, Tim," I said.

"I am, this would be the biggest win of my career."

I slapped him on the shoulder and told him to relax as we headed inside. There were large signs and posters on the wall with my name and slogan. The crowd was already standing at attention as we shook hands and hugged everyone.

Out of the corner of my eye, I saw Gage, Nina, Maya, and Talbot, standing in the front of the podium.

"The numbers are coming in, and so far, you have the Brooklyn and Bronx districts. You're in the lead by twenty points. Do you need water or anything?" Scottie asked.

"I need Maya," I replied, and she smiled and pointed for me to go ahead over to her.

Strolling over to my woman, I hugged her tight, kissing the side of her neck and spinning her around. She was looking delectable in a light pink one-shoulder dress with minimal skin showing and her hair up in a bun.

"I want to take you right here, but at the same time I'd hate to kill anyone that looked at you," I groaned in her ear, kissing her lips as the cameras went off. I didn't care who knew we were an item because she belonged to me.

"Calm down, cowboy. First, the opening speech and then a treat," Maya insisted, pulling away from me, trying to walk over to the girls.

"What's wrong?"

"Nothing, you have an election to win, and I have work to do so go be great and we'll catch up in a little bit." She stood on her tippy toes and kissed me on the lips.

"Stay close," I demanded, kissing her one more time and letting her go over to her FBX team.

My mother passed me a napkin to wipe the lipstick off as more numbers came rolling in. I could hear the reporters say that I was surging in the lead, and they could already tell that I had won and became the new governor of New York.

Screams of joy and celebratory yells were heard throughout the room. Scottie ran on stage with Genesis, Celine, Tailynn, and the entire crew hugging me.

The only person I wanted by my side was off in the corner, getting a mic for a story.

"Speech! Speech!" the room demanded.

"Honestly, I'm overwhelmed and floored you've chosen me. First, I want to say thank you to Robert Lanton; he was a tough and honest candidate to be up against, and I respect him more for wanting to better New York. Second, I want to thank my family and friends, for not only working on my campaign and helping me to get to this place but believing in what we can do for the future of New York. Gage and Talbot, without you two listening to me complain every other day, I wouldn't have a leg to stand on. Maya, you've dealt with the long nights of being away and the crazy media attention that you didn't ask for. I truly thank you for sticking with me. To all of New York, there's work to be done, so let's go," I yelled, clapping my hands, as the theme music of Bruce was playing in the background. We stood up there for hours, taking pictures, and talking with supporters.

Maya was finally able to get her interview for her show, and we sat in the back of the limo headed to my home. I ran a hand across her thigh as she looked out the window.

"What are you thinking?"

"How things are going to change for us," she answered, smiling at me, but it didn't seem to meet her eyes.

"If we stay focused on us, I promise not to let the craziness get to us."

The car pulled up to my house, and we went inside and headed to bed.

Maya undressed in the bathroom. She usually didn't care if I saw her naked. I felt like she was tugging away from me. I began to regret the last few weeks and months where I held back from fighting for something I never knew I wanted. A relationship that I didn't want to die out.

Chapter 25

Ethan

I stood under the shower as the water ran down. We'd come back late from celebrating my nomination as governor of New York. All night my phone was blowing up, and the media automatically stationed outside of my gated home as soon as my name was announced. Ten minutes later, I dried off, grabbing a pair of pants and shirt to change into as the men downstairs continued moving my things. Maya left extra early without telling me and was ignoring my calls and messages. I slammed the phone down on my bed, heading out of my bedroom into my office, where I saw Tim on the phone.

"He just walked in, okay, bye."

"What are you doing here?" I queried.

"You need to make up your mind, Ethan. Things like this won't work now that you're the Governor," Tim explained as I stood with my hands in my pockets, while Garret was pulling out files to box up.

"What are you talking about?"

"Leaving on a whim with Maya. You're the governor

now, you need to have a detail with you at all times. I spoke with the commissioner, and we have a list of people that will be assigned to you once you move in to the governor's mansion."

"Sorry."

"Sorry, you do realize that at any moment, if anything happens to you, this was all for nothing?" Tim insisted.

"You're right, I apologize, tell the mayor and commissioner I will not leave again without having my security with me. Did you see Maya this morning when you came in?"

"No, why?"

"Nothing."

"Please tell me there are no issues with you two already?"

"Tim, you worry too much."

"Well, we need to get you packed and headed over to the swearing-in, and you have a host of meetings today with the mayor and other messages to return calls to other leaders in government," Tim said.

"Okay, can I at least eat first?" I teased.

"Garret ordered you a coffee and bagel already. It's in the kitchen. We need to go."

Grabbing my keys and wallet, I followed Tim and Garret, grabbing my coffee and bagel, before leaving for the day to get my official first day as governor started. I'd call Maya later on for lunch.

Chapter 26

Maya

"What are you going to do?" Nina said.

"I need a drink," I said, getting to my feet. Normally, you wouldn't catch me in sweats and my hair all over the place. Since finding out I was pregnant, the thought of being someone's mother terrified me.

I left Ethan's place super early once he fell asleep. Walter saw me leaving and knew what was bothering me. Standing with my girls, we looked at the contracts from California and Seattle and deliberated on what I should do.

"I think you need to talk with Ethan," Scottie spoke.

"You're saying that because he's your friend."

"He's your man. I've been there, Maya. Running won't make the decision any less hard. You need to face him and find out how you both can compromise with the new dynamics of your lives. He's not going to let you run away with his baby."

"I know, Scottie, but I need some time to think and get my head on straight. You and Genesis had a different situation than us. We weren't in a serious relationship until recently, and I don't need the media thinking I'm trying to pin a baby on the newly elected governor and I sure as hell won't be some crazy baby momma. I have goals and plans for myself."

"Nina, please talk to her," Kasey spoke.

"She has it in her head that she knows what's best, and we can't fight her on it for anything. I'll tell you that we as your friends support you and want you to be happy, and if that includes going off to who knows where without any friends or family with you as back up, then I'm happy for you, best friend," Nina condescendingly remarked.

"I truly appreciate my friends," I mumbled to myself.

* * *

Two days later

Nina was driving me to the airport as I wiped my tears. I tried to stay active and not let it get to me. There was only so much I could deal with as the girlfriend of the governor. Ethan was meant for great things, and I'm not the sharing type of woman. The public was too invasive, and I hated the constant hounding and people parked outside of my place and my parents' home. Even though I hadn't spoken with my mom, I didn't want anything bad happening to her.

"We're here," Nina stated, parking the car at the curb for drop off.

"Thanks, Nina. I'm sorry you don't like my decision, but I have to make this move for myself."

"Maya, you're my girl, I would never fault you for wanting to further your career. At the same time, I'll never be the kind of friend that tells you yes all the time. Keep in touch, and you visit as much as possible," Nina commented.

I started to give her another hug when my door was yanked open, and we both screamed in fear. Two large burly men stood with earpieces in their ear and black suits talking into their mic.

I sucked my teeth because I already knew who was behind this. "Ma'am, please come with me."

"No," I spat.

"Is this necessary?" Nina questioned.

He nodded and pointed to the black SUV behind us.

"What do you want to do? Because I can still drive off and head up north with you, we'd just be some criminals on the road," Nina stated.

The both of us cackled at her idea of Thelma and Louise-ing it.

"It's better that you don't, ma'am; he has all the airports shut down and roads closed," the security guard said, holding a hand out for me to take.

"Damn, girl, you must have put that fire on his ass," Nina laughed.

"Same as you with Gage."

"Go and see what he wants and call me. We can always change your flight."

"Thanks, Nina, I'll call you later if the warden lets me." I stepped out of the car with my bags and walked over to the black tinted SUV.

The door opened, and he sat inside furthest to the window, not looking at me.

Jumping in and buckling my seatbelt, he advised the driver to leave.

"Who told you?"

"Your fucking ex-boy toy, Douglas!"

"Listen Ethan-"

Before I could finish, he held a hand up for me to be quiet and we rode in silence around to the back entrance of the airport with the private jets.

"Where are you taking me?"

"Get out and we'll talk on the plane."

The door opened, and the same security guard helped me out and escorted us to the private plane. Dropping my bags on the seat, I buckled up and waited for his instructions.

"Why did I hear from Douglas that not only are you leaving out of town for a new job but that you're pregnant, Maya, with my child? When did I become the enemy?"

"Ethan, I never wanted you to feel like I was a burden on you because of me getting pregnant. Douglas found out from Tonya because she wanted my job. She told him once I rejected him and his ego was bruised. I was going to tell you about the baby when I cleared my head," I stated.

"I would never hide my family, nor do I feel like you're a burden. I don't run my life like that, and I wouldn't ask you to do that either. You need to understand that making decisions isn't a *you* thing anymore; it's a *we* thing as in the *both* of us," Ethan challenged, squeezing my hand in comfort.

Chapter 27

Ethan

We escaped to my cabin out of the city to be alone and avoid the paparazzi. I called it West Farms. It was two hundred acres of land. It had a barn in the back with horses, cows, chickens, and my dog, Pickle, as well as a guest house for visitors.

I did have Carol fax over some paperwork that needed my attention, but it could wait once Maya and I talked. I had to do something to stop her before she got on that plane. Finding out she was pregnant from that lowlife Douglas and not her, pissed me off. I almost caused a fight at the station, which would have caused bigger problems. Getting Hannah arrested for stalking and trying to hurt Maya was another task within itself. Seemed like everyone was trying to keep us apart. Two people that we never promised we'd be in a relationship with caused the problems next to us not being honest with each other.

She hadn't woken yet, and I was hesitant to disturb her; she was cranky if you woke her up too early. Sitting in a chair, sipping coffee, I watched her chest move up and down.

"Why are you watching me sleep?" Maya grumbled while waking up, letting the blanket fall just below her plump breasts in the nightgown.

"When were you going to tell me?" I asked.

"Once I settled in Seattle, I would've told you about the baby, Ethan." She jumped up, stubbornly throwing the covers off and stomped into the bathroom.

"Hormones," I chided.

"What was that?" Maya poked her head out with a toothbrush in her mouth.

Standing up, I slowly strode into the bathroom with my chest to her back. Closing the space between us as she rinsed her mouth out, our eyes locked onto each other as we both smiled in the mirror. Running a hand up and down her arm, I leaned in close kissing the back of her neck.

"I would never keep your child away from you, Ethan. I just needed time to gather my thoughts and figure out what this meant for me. Having a child was not in my plans for my future."

Sighing, I turned her around, and she reached up, clasping her hands around my neck.

Bending down, I branded her neck with kisses. Squeezing her body to mine, with a groan, I slipped a hand from her neck down her back to her ass, pressing each plump cheek.

"Get on the bed," I demanded, smacking her ass. There was something so tender about her actions as she grasped my hand, leading me to the bed, crawling up to the middle, motioning for me to come to her. I was joining her in bed, a fury and flash of desire tightened in my gut. I had to be gentle, to not hurt the baby.

"Ethan, please." I was tracing a sensuous path from her chest to her sweet ecstasy. She squirmed beneath the thin fabric.

She lay panting, her chest heaving as I slid her panties to the side and tasted her warm, sweet, heaven.

"Mhmmm...baby." She caressed the back of my head as I tortured her with my tongue, lapping up her juices.

"Arghhh! Yes... right there."

This was the time for us to reconnect as my hands roamed intimately over her breasts, before I quickly slid a finger in her asshole as I flattened my tongue. She gasped in sweet agony.

"Fuck!... Baby, you squirted," I complimented.

"Ohhh, *God*!" She cried out for release as I watched her drench the bed, letting her taste herself. She pulled me up for a kiss. Hovering over her body, I placed my dick at her entrance and eased inside. We both groaned at the same time.

She welcomed me home. The pleasure was pure and explosive. I desperately needed more of her and never wanted to remove myself.

"Shit! You're tight." I cocked my head to the side from her to the floor, trying to compose myself so I wouldn't come too early.

Rotating my hips, I held a steady pace as her legs wrapped around my waist.

She rubbed up and down my back, kissing me gently on the cheek, lips, and shoulder.

"Ughh.... fuck, Maya," I moaned.

The bed started to squeak, and our groans became louder.

"Fuck me," she insisted.

Something inside of her unleashed, and she didn't want gentle tonight. Maya wanted me to own her body and soul. Rotating our positions, I guided her on top of me to take what she needed.

"Ethannn...baby."

She leaned down, nuzzling her nose in my neck as I spanked her ass again. She flattened her feet on the bed and started rocking back and forth. She bit her lip hard around the smile that tugged at her mouth. Squeezing her own breast, I captured the right one, licking and squeezing as she did the same to the left.

Meeting her stroke for stroke, she almost came until I turned us again and had her facing the headboard.

"Put him back in, damn it," Maya snapped, trying to grip my dick while smacking the bed. Ignoring her pleading, I feasted on my favorite meal. "Mhmm!" I moaned.

Wanting to be back inside of her I moved up, sliding my dick back in and started thrusting. Right as we both were coming, she pushed me away and took my dick in her mouth.

"What the fuck! Maya," I shouted, gripping her hair as she sucked my entire soul out of my body. Her touch sent tingles up my arm. She reached over to grab the handcuffs out of the drawer and reached back over, locking my hands to the headboard.

"My turn," she quipped, seductively riding the head of my dick at a slow pace.

Chapter 28

Ethan

Three days later, I was back in the city, reading over bills that had been left on my desk that had piled up. I planned on proposing to Maya later tonight at her birthday party on the boat. She didn't suspect anything, and I had Scottie and Nina help keep her busy today with shopping and a spa day.

Carol walked inside, carrying my lunch. "Mr. West, I have Genesis on line one."

I picked up the call, mouthing *thank you* as she walked back out.

"Hello, Mr. West."

"Genesis, how are you doing?"

"Everything is good. Checking in about the party tonight and making sure you're still going through with your plans?"

"Yep. She has no idea and thank Scottie again for keeping her busy today. Earlier she was complaining about having to go out because she's tired from the pregnancy and I had to bribe her to get her out of the house."

"Yeah, get used to the hormones, it's only the beginning. Scottie was up and down with her hormones when she was pregnant."

"Maya is so cranky and complaining every second about my cologne—which is something she said she loved about me in the first place." I chuckled to myself, remembering our first official date after the hotel.

"I saw the headlines about the Hannah situation. Press is still holding on to the stalker situation."

Closing out of my computer, I signed off on the final details for the groundbreaking legislation for a STEM school program across the city. "It's taking everything in me not to call in some favors and get the story buried, but that would only cause more problems for myself with her family. They're trying to say it wasn't her that did all those things. I'm more focused on getting the proposal right and keeping Maya from throwing up on a boat tonight," I chortled as I grabbed my jacket and briefcase heading out of the office.

"Genesis, let me call you back from the car. I have a meeting with the Lt. Governor in twenty minutes about the teachers strike looming."

"No rush, see you tonight. And Ethan?"

"Yeah."

"As a married man, you no longer get to be the bossy one in the relationship. It's all about compromise, my friend. Look at Gage; no one would have ever expected him to calm down and get married. But love has a way of changing you. Once you finish, you should come hang out with the guys. I have friends in town I'd like to introduce you to."

"Who?" I questioned, stepping out of the building, and stepping into the limousine.

"Chance, a friend from Australia. He's here in town for a visit."

"Bring him to the party. The more people the better. That would probably keep Maya from saying no to my marriage proposal."

The driver pulled off into traffic, heading to the Department of Education for the meeting.

My phone vibrated, and I saw a text message from Maya. It was a picture of her in a robe and facial mask. Hanging up with Genesis, I texted Maya that she looked edible, with a heart emoji and a tongue emoji.

I didn't wait for the driver to open the door. I stepped out myself, meeting the superintendent at the door. Education was important to me, and with Maya about to have our child, I wanted to give every child a fair shot at getting a good education with the best teachers. Making sure those teachers were compensated fairly was one of my campaign promises.

"Good afternoon, Governor West." Amanda reached her hand out for a shake.

I returned her greeting. We walked inside to get the meeting started.

* * *

Four hours after the meeting I was sitting in the car with Maya heading to the boat for her birthday party. She wore a short strapless black dress that ruffled at the bottom, as well as a pair of high heel shoes that I protested the moment I saw them because if she fell and hurt herself or the baby, I would lose my mind.

"Thank you, baby."

"For what?" I asked, snuggling her into my side as best as I could with the seatbelt separating us.

"For loving me and letting me see that you're not a grumpy guy like the press makes you out to be. I love that you don't scare easily when it comes to me and you challenge me like no other man has." Maya grasped my hand, squeezing softly. I kissed the back of her hand.

"How was the spa?"

"It was fun, Nina and Scottie drove me crazy with their back and forth ranting about having dinner ready for the kids after the game today. Remind me once I have this baby to not turn into a mom that spends every waking moment thinking about my child," Maya sighed, laying her head back on the headrest.

When we arrived at the dock, the driver came around and opened the door for Maya, and I stepped out behind her, buttoning my jacket. She leaned lightly against me. I helped her step onto the boat. It was decked out with lights hanging around the sides and a sign that read, "Happy Birthday," while a band was playing old-school R&B classics. Our closest friends and family were gathered together.

"Maya, happy birthday, bestie!" Nina exclaimed.

"This is nice, Ethan. The last time I was on a boat, it was on a girls' cruise, baby. Thank you," she said, turning around and finding me on my knees holding a ring.

The entire boat got quiet as she stood in shock. I moved her hand away from her face as tears started to fall down.

"Baby."

"Omg! Is this happening? Wait, how..."

"Maya Armstrong, you are the most beautiful woman I have ever met. Since you've been in my life, you've driven me up a wall with your stubbornness, smart mouth, and sexy..."

She cut me off with her hand over my mouth. Chuckling at her reaction, I kissed the back of her hand, holding the ring up.

"I would be honored to be the husband of Maya Armstrong, if you'll have me?" I asked, staring intensely into her eyes as they welled up with tears.

She nodded, dropping to her knees, kissing me on the lips.

"Is that a yes?" I questioned, pulling back.

"Yes! I'd love to marry you," she answered, sliding the ring on her finger.

All of our friends and family came over to hug and kiss us. Maya's parents rushed her, along with her sister.

"Maya, I'm so happy for you. You look beautiful, girl. You know I need this dress, cousin," Lauren said. They started alongside one another in the business. She's now on her way to the top as a makeup reviewer. More name-brand cosmetics are knocking on her door to have her as an influencer.

"Thanks, Lauren, so happy you came. How is everything going with you? Kasey, you look gorgeous, and I like the hair. Short looks good on you," Maya replied.

As the girls mixed and mingled, her mother walked over with her father behind her.

"Maya, I'm proud of you, baby," her father said, placing a kiss on her forehead.

"Thanks, Dad, did you know about this?"

"I did, and I'm very impressed with him; he came to your mother and me about wanting to marry you. I told him you're precious to our family, so he better not mess up or I'll come take care of him," my father joked.

Hazel, her mother, stepped in front of her, and said, "You look gorgeous, Maya. I'm very happy for you."

"Thanks."

Clearing her throat, she said, "I wanted to apologize to you, and I know this won't be an easy road. But I would like to start over with our relationship. These past few months, I started seeing a therapist."

"Wow, hmm."

"You don't have to answer me right now. Please enjoy your night, and Ethan, thank you for loving our daughter," Hazel said, hugging me and walking off with her father.

Emery, Nina, and Diya came over to congratulate us. "Ethan, you better not hurt our friend or we're going to come looking for you. We know where you work," Emery joked.

"I promise I'll take care of her heart forever," I said.

The waiters came over and passed us all champagne. Genesis, Scottie and Gage joined us.

"Bro, welcome to the husband club," Gage stated.

I extended a hand to Genesis. "Ethan, you finally worked up the courage to bring your woman back," Genesis said.

"I had to, man. She wasn't getting away from me that easy," I responded, squeezing Maya to my side.

"Scottie, did you help him pick out the ring, because I'm impressed?" Maya inquired, showing her ring off to the group.

The band started playing "Single Ladies," and the girls gathered in a group to start dancing. I stood to the side, watching with the other guys as they all danced and cheered her on. As the night went on, we ate and drank together until three a.m.

Chapter 29

Maya

Spotlight *with Maya Armstrong* was playing on the TV. I watched myself say, "I want to thank you all for watching me this season, and I cannot wait to continue this journey with you as the First Lady of the state of New York. For now, I'm taking a few months off to enjoy this new phase, and I will be back to give you more fabulous content—just a little less gossipy."

"Turn that off," Ethan demanded as he gripped my hip, easing in at an even pace. He moved to kiss a path down my stomach.

"Baby..." he groaned, claiming my breast with his hand. Ever since my pregnancy, I've been hornier than I've ever been in my life. I needed it at least three or more times a day. It was to the point that he had to add it to his schedule. No matter where he was, he had to have me with him, and I was his priority if I had an itch that needed scratching.

He admired my stomach, smiling as he pushed inside me again.

"Ooh... yes, baby."

"Shit. You feel that?"

I nodded in answer. I leaned up to grasp his face and run my tongue across his lips.

"Never question how much I love you. Do...you...hear me, Maya?" Ethan lifted my chin staring into my eyes.

Smiling in answer, I maneuvered him onto his back, straddling him with my back to his chest.

Placing my feet flat on the bed, he gripped my waist as I lined his fat dick up with my wet pussy. The warmth radiated off me and before I eased further down on him, I was leaking on him and the sheets as I bounced up and down slowly.

"Ahhhh... fuck."

"Go slow."

"Shit... Ethan."

The throbbing between my thighs overwhelmed me. He growled at the ferocity of the pleasure that ripped through him.

"I'm in control this time, Ethan."

"Mmmm... Maya... fuck. What are you doing to me?" He slapped my ass.

I bent over even farther, until I was just fucking his tip.

"Ah... oh, my God!"

* * *

Three hours later

The party was getting full and everyone was dancing and having a good time. Talbot had a booth where he was face painting the kids. Gage had a small batting cage section going against Tailynn, chuckling at her trying to push her dad out of the way for cheating.

Our friends walked over to us.

"Congrats again. Maya, you're looking beautiful as ever," Genesis said, bending down to give me hug.

"Thanks, Genesis. What about doing that interview for my show?"

"From what I've seen, your interviews don't turn out so well for the guests you have."

"What do you mean?"

Genesis scratched the back of his neck in nervousness and Scottie leaned into him, placing a kiss on his cheek grinning.

"We all saw that interview with Gage, and then you and Ethan. I don't need to have my life dissected on live TV."

I waved him off. "The interview with Gage was more of an exposè. He understood and forgave me. Later on, we came to an understanding. The interview with Ethan was me doing my job as a journalist."

"Maya, you asked Ethan if he wears boxers or briefs!"

"That's like asking whom you would rather have a beer with: Bush or Obama."

I just have a more direct in-depth version," I responded, shrugging my shoulders.

"You really believe that? Ethan, good luck with this one."

"Hey, leave my pregnant friend alone. Besides, he asked her to marry him, so she's not *that* crazy," Scottie jested.

"Whose side are you on, Scottie?" I questioned, craning my neck to the side with hands on my hips.

She reached out to hug me, stating, "Yours, bestie."

"Uh... huh. Anyway, you men leave us alone. I need to talk with my girls."

"We'll be over by the pool. Call me if you need anything, baby." Ethan gestured toward Celine and Tailynn kicking the water in the pool.

I nodded.

Nina and Nicole walked over, and we all sat under the canopy.

"I don't see how you guys deal with being pregnant," I said. "I'm done after this, I swear."

"Maya you're only two months, not showing, and you're complaining," Nicole said dryly.

"Nina complained when she was pregnant, so did Scottie. I deserve to complain."

She waved me off as Tailynn and Celine walked over toward us.

Tailynn wrapped her arm around Nina's left leg and peered over at Scottie, before she asked, "Auntie Scottie, can I spend the night with Celine tonight?"

"If your mom says it's okay. I don't mind."

"Did you ask your dad, Tailynn?" Nina inquired.

Tailynn nodded in answer.

"I can see now if we have a girl, Ethan's going to be so territorial, it's a shame. How does Genesis deal with Celine growing up?" I questioned.

"Genesis doesn't want to think about her dating or growing up too fast," Genesis stated from behind us. "She's still obsessed with *Sesame Street*. Let's leave it at that for now."

Ethan followed and wrapped his arms around my waist, kissing me on the lips.

"It's pretty ironic that Gage and Nina got together because of Genesis's fundraiser, and now Maya and Ethan are together and about to get married because of Genesis's charity event. So, it seems as though Genesis's yearly events are good-luck charms for all his friends," Diya commented.

"Oh, maybe Scottie and Genesis can hook me up for next year?" Nicole enthusiastically shared, jumping up and down and clapping her hands.

"No!" we all shouted at the same time.

"Genesis is retiring from throwing fundraising events," Genesis said.

"Why are you talking in third person?" Scottie responded, enveloping Genesis's right arm. He bent down, kissed her cheek, and rubbed his hand up and down her back.

"Hanging around your friends too long. Sorry, Nicole, maybe Maya can fix you up with someone from Ethan's office."

"Nicole is too flakey, and besides I'd rather she not be around all those young fresh single men at your office."

"Why not?" Ethan questioned, his hands buried deep in his pockets.

"Because the second she runs up there showing off her singledom, all her single friends will end up hanging out and trying to seduce you. I think not," I fumed narrowing my eyes at Nicole as she gleefully shrugged.

Ethan smiled that sexy smile and pulled me into his chest, before he whispered in my ear. "No woman will have my toes curling like you do, babe." Ethan lifted my chin kissing me deeply.

I relaxed, sinking into his cushioning embrace. The touch of his lips was a devious sensation.

"Can you two control yourselves?" Nina fussed, covering Tailynn and Celine's eyes.

We both pulled away from each other, clearing our throats.

"Uhm, Ethan, I'm not feeling very well. I think I need to go rest for a few minutes," I remarked, running a hand over my stomach, looking around at all the snickering faces, not really caring if they knew I was faking being sick.

"You are not sick, lady," Diya chastised, shaking her head in dismay.

"I blame you, Ethan, she's spoiled rotten and can you just imagine when she gets further along how hard it'll be to turn her down?" Scottie bit her lip to stifle a grin.

He spread his hands regretfully and shrugged. "Can Genesis ever turn you down?"

Genesis's infectious grin set the tone. "Don't answer that, Genesis," Scottie said.

These two were hilarious.

"Are you coming, Ethan?" I asked, turning to walk away as he followed behind me.

"What about my job, Ethan?" Nicole yelled.

"Nicole, you've had three jobs in one year from an office clerk at the community center, sex toy worker, DJ, and now you want to work at the governor's office? Do I have that right?" I asked.

She replied with a nod.

"Nicole, we love you, boo, but Ethan's trying to have a no scandal year in the governor's mansion and the last thing we need is you trying to turn his office into a nightclub."

"Coming from the gossip queen," Nicole groaned, sitting down on the patio chair.

"Don't harp on my woman. Nicole, come down to my office on Monday and we'll talk. Maya, let's go you've been out here on your feet all day," Ethan said.

"Okay, honey."

As we started to walk back into the house, we noticed a guy walking up toward us waving. "Ethan, how are you?" Chance reached his hand out to shake.

"Who are you?"

He stood tall and straight like a towering spruce with a body of a surfer boy. "I'm a friend of Scottie and Genesis. Chance... "

His stood there looking devilishly handsome.

"Hey, Chance, thanks for coming," Scottie said.

"Scottie, thanks for inviting me, nice place you have here. Ethan and Maya, right?" he stated, shaking Ethan's hand.

"Thanks, hang out and enjoy yourself," Ethan said, placing his arm around my shoulder.

"Hello, I'm Nicole and I'm single," Nicole stated, flirting in front of everyone.

"Nooo!!!" we all shouted at the same time, removing Nicole's hands out of Chance's. Scottie pushed Nicole behind her and took Chance over to the table of food.

"I guess she's giving you some payback," Nina implied.

"Funny, I don't recall ever behaving like her to get a man," I said nonchalantly.

Ethan arched a brow. "I love it when you think you've been innocent through all of this. But that's a story for another day, baby."

We both laughed together at his comment, walking hand in hand back into the house.

Epilogue: Ethan

Usually, she'd help me run over my speech before any major speeches. She was sitting over on the opposite end of the couch doing a crossword puzzle. Something we both had in common that I found out when we started dating. It became a Sunday afternoon ritual after we married. I promised her as things got busier for me in the governorship, I would set every Saturday as date night, and Sunday for family.

We spent the day at the park with the kids, then visited our families, and then came back home putting the kids to bed and sitting together alone catching up with everything that had been going on in our careers. She still did her talk show, *Spotlight with Maya* part-time and had Nina's little sister Nicole as a fill-in whenever she had something with the kids, or they were sick and she needed to stay home. We had a nanny and housekeeper too. According to Maya, what was the point in having a billionaire for a husband if she couldn't spend the money to hire the help so she could continue keeping up her fabulous appearance?

I put the speech down on the table and reached over to grab her feet. She moaned lowly as I massaged and kissed the palm and top of her right toe. She wiggled her foot in my hands and I smiled, catching a little grin spread across her face. Maya Armstrong-West, the cocky, sassy, stubborn, no love only sex type of girl was an Executive Producer of her own show and owner of the station. Now that she was my wife, I gifted her as a wedding present the entire station that aired her talk show. She eventually started creating more shows to air either before hers or after. She was becoming a mogul in her own right and still took care of home as the First Lady of New York and the mother of three kids. Our son, Ethan, Jr., was three years old going on four, and big brother to twin siblings, Eric and Erika West. The two-year-old twins looked exactly like Maya. At one time Maya was ready to leave and move to Los Angeles for a career opportunity. Both of us being stubborn and not admitting our feelings would have caused all of this to never exist.

"What's floating around in that head of yours, Mr. West?" Maya asked as I took the crossword out of her hands and placed it on the side table next to us. I laid her flat on her back and she opened her legs wide for me to squeeze in between with my hand rubbing up her leg, then thigh.

"You," I spoke, staring into her eyes. Recently she'd cut her hair into a short bob. I didn't mind if it was long or short, only if I could pull on it during sex. Which she hated at times, but the way she had me moaning and groaning during sex, I couldn't help myself but to try and grip her hair to move her off me. What I loved most about her was that she wasn't like the other political wives we'd seen in the past or currently. Maya was her own woman, with goals and dreams. She didn't need me to be who she'd become. To her, I was a bonus in her life, and I realized I needed her more than she even knew. It gave me hope for the next fifty years that our lives would never be boring. It also didn't hurt that she's quick to call me on my shit and challenge me at every turn compared to people at my office or the media that sometimes became yes men to please me. Maya was the complete opposite. We've laughed often that the only reason they voted me in was because of Maya and how the public liked her more than me and if given the choice, they'd prefer she run as the next governor of New York.

"What about me, Mr. Governor?" She leaned up to kiss me on the corner of my mouth, then pecked my lips slowly.

"Thinking of how we started from a one-night stand, and me not remembering you. Then you being friends with Nina, Scottie, Genesis, and Gage. I feel like it's a small circle. On top of that the public probably only voted me in because of you," I answered, kissing the top of her forehead.

"Daddy! Daddy!" Ethan, Jr., Eric, and Erika all came running inside the study room. Living at the governor's mansion we had some things updated with a treehouse built in the backyard, added a playroom for the kids, and a little fun room for me and Maya that only us two had the key to that held some special toys we started to collect. During our early time of dating, she kept a drawer of sex toys next to her bed and I wanted her to continue to feel free enough to explore our sex life and not feel less sexual now that we had kids. Nina told me at one point she was not feeling as beautiful because of back-to-back having kids. Every chance I got, I put in the time to let her know I found her beautiful not only on the inside, but outside as well.

Our little girl was a daddy's girl and Ethan, Jr. stayed under his mother at all times. Eric was the loner and didn't need to be under us the way his siblings tended to be. Like now, Erika pushed Maya away from me and tried to climb in my lap.

"Esque..my Daddy," Erika said as she reached out for me to pick her up. I smirked before I picked her up, kissed her cheek, then placed her in my lap so she could show me her new dolly.

"She's so rude," Maya said.

"Don't be jealous, baby," I replied as Ethan and Eric sat in front of the table with their Lego blocks trying to build a castle.

"You spoil her, Ethan," Maya amusedly said standing to her feet and stretching her arms.

"I spoil both my girls," I stated, capturing her wrist, and pulling her back down on the couch, wrapping my arm around her shoulder, before leaning to whisper into her ear. "Don't pout, baby, I'll spoil you later with my tongue," I commented, kissing the side of her neck, ear, and cheek. She giggled and reached over to squeeze Erika's cheek.

"Before or after you make a decision?" She sighed nervously.

"Just say the word and I won't do it."

"I would never make a decision like that for you, babe. I trust you'll protect our family and keep us safe. It's your choice, let me take Erika and the boys to get them ready for bed. You finish with your work." Maya grabbed Erika who yawned as Maya patted her back.

If I was being honest with myself, I was nervous about

this next step and if I should really commit. The amount of time it's taken away from me not tucking my kids in at night still made me nervous. At the same time, we've made great strides in the city and I'm ready to continue to see what more we could do on a bigger platform. Looking toward the door Ethan, Jr., and Eric followed behind their mother. "Maya," I said, stopping her in her tracks. She knew what I was about to say.

"Yes, Mr. President?" Maya answered amusedly. I winked in acknowledgement that I was taking the step in my career to help as many people as I could. What's the point in having all this money if I couldn't help more people? I planned to put my money to good use with not running for governorship for another four years, but as President of the United States and Maya Armstrong-West as the First Lady.

"After you tuck the kids in bed, meet me in the bedroom so I can tuck you in properly," I answered honestly, and she blushed blowing a kiss back to me as the kids ran off upstairs to their rooms. I turned around in my seat and picked up the glass of scotch on the table, before I picked up my pen and official paperwork announcing my intention to run for president, signing on the bottom line with my name, Ethan West.

"Here's to the next four years," I stated to myself raising the glass in the air.

* * *

I hope you enjoyed **Ethan** and **Maya**, if you want to see more of these character check out bonus scenes here "https://chiquitadennie.squarespace.com/bonus-scenes , Follow TN Seal Security series with a standalone, opposites attract, fake dating, military romance "**Nicco**" https://bit.ly/47ZZN6p Are you a fan of sports romance? Then download one-night stand, billionaire romance "**Refuel**"https://bit.ly/3RqFx8l Also, follow it up with workplace, sports romance "**Pressure**" https://bit.ly/3RqagT1 If you love romantic comedy, fake relationships, enemies to lovers, find it here, "**Something Gained.**" Click the link https://bit.ly/3OwGbiP. My stories of friends finding love started with the Heart of Stone series that includes a host of characters and family. "**Broken**" book 1 Emery and Jackson a sports, one night stand, workplace romance is here:https://bit.ly/3hxVavF

Then you can continue with a fun side story of Emery and Jackson with "**Valentine's Day short** here:https://bit.ly/42ttg7o

Jordan, her best friend's story, continues here in "**Rebirth**" book 2 a single dad, widow billionaire romance here:https://bit.ly/3YiQtGS Hope on and download "**Reveal**" with Angela and Brent https://bit.ly/3OupYur If you love bonus content click here "https://chiquitadennie.squarespace.com/bonus-scenes

* * *

Please also check out a second-chance workplace romance here, "**Renew Book 4**"https://bit.ly/3worgHi with a host of characters intertwined.

Follow Desiree and Gabriel in "**Temptation**" a standalone contemporary, sports, curvy girl romance. Check it out herehttps://bit.ly/42r8ODQ

Check out dark mafia romance here that started my

journey with Antonio and Sabrina in "**Ruthless Book 1**"https://bit.ly/3iS64XT

The relationship continues in "**Savage**" book 2 as they get to know each other and their families:https://bit.ly/3w77CJT

Antonio and Sabrina have more work to do in "**Beast**" book 3 right here:https://bit.ly/3Untivm

* * *

Did you know **Janice** and **Carlo** have a book? Well grab this dark mafia romance with emotional scars, and betrayal right here:https://bit.ly/42yJBaH

Any fans of forbidden romance, political? Check out "**Mutual Agreement**"https://bit.ly/3OyAzod a steamy romance. Do you love workplace romantic suspense? Then check out "**Aydin**" https://bit.ly/496jKcv and the interconnected standalone hate to love, actress, damsel in distress bodyguard romance "**Nasir**" click the link here https://bit.ly/3uovwQr

Have you checked out "**She's All I Need**" click here https://books2read.com/u/49lkeW a sports, opposites attract romance. What about dark romance that has everything from steamy romance, opposites attract, suspense, thriller, celebrity, and more "**Stolen Book 1**" https://books2read.com/u/mvZlgV Don't miss the follow up Joaquin and Sofia's story in book 2 "**Saved**" https://books2read.com/u/4DWwLd

The conclusion for Joaquin and Sofia comes full circle in "**Betrayed**" here: https://books2read.com/u/4A5LGp

* * *

Catch up with favorite characters in this holiday short romance which includes spoilers. "**Holiday collection**" here https://books2read.com/u/bzd59G

For small town, single mom stories check out "**Until Seren**a" https://books2read.com/u/mej8vr. Always fun when you love billionaire romances so check in with "**Cocky Catcher**" a sports romance, enemies to lovers here https://bit.ly/3R57VeT

A reader of sports workplace romance? Grab "**Scoring with Sadie**" a workplace, enemies to lovers romance here:https://bit.ly/3nkWhBp All curvy girl, plus size romance lovers get into "**I Deserve His Love**" a standalone, second chance romance here: https://books2read.com/u/mVrGwP

The fantasy romance readers look no further than a "**Red Light District**" a curvy girl, fling romance here: https://books2read.com/u/m2RQ6G

Spotify Playlist

1. Faith Evans Love: Like This Before
2. Fantasia- When I see U
3. Ella Mai- Boo'd Up
4. Bruno Mars- That's What I Like
5. Usher- There Goes My Baby
6. Shania Twain- That Don't Impress Me Much
7. Faith Hill& Tim McGraw- Lets Make Love
8. Ne-Yo-Miss Independent
9. J.Lo- Get Right
10. Beyonce-Upgrade U

Heart of Stone Universe

Broken 1 Emery and Jackson
https://books2read.com/u/boWPAV
Heart of Stone Book 1.5
https://payhip.com/b/kWg7
Rebirth 2 Jordan and Damon
https://books2read.com/u/ba2OMx
Heart of Stone Book 3.5 Bottoms Up
https://payhip.com/b/HGP1
Reveal 3 Angela and Brent
https://books2read.com/u/31rx9l
Renew 4 Jessica and Joseph
https://books2read.com/u/4NXyPG

Also By Chiquita Dennie

Series

Struck in Love

The Early Years-A Prequel Short Story
Ruthless:Antonio and Sabrina Book 1
Savage: Antonio and Sabrina Book 2
Beastl: Antonio and Sabrina Book 3
Captivated By His Love:Janice and Carlo
Brutal: Antonio and Sabrina Booke 4
Redemption: Antonio and Sabrina Book 5

Heart of Stone

Broken, Book 1 (Emery & Jackson)
A Valentine's Day Short Book 1.5 Emery & Jackson
Rebirth, Book 2 (Jordan and Damon)
Reveal, Book 3 (Angela and Brent)
Bottoms Up Book 3.5 Jessica and Joseph Short
Renew, Book 4 (Jessica and Joseph)

Cocky Billionaire Boys

Cocky Catcher (Cocky Billionaire Boys Book 1)
Bossy Billionaire (Cocky Billionaire Boys Book 2)

The Fuertes Cartel

Stolen (The Fuertes Cartel Book 1)
Saved (The Fuertes Cartel Book 2)
Betrayed (The Fuertes Cartel Book 3)

Carrington Cartel

Torn: The Carrington Cartel Book 1
Claim: The Carrington Cartel Book 2

Something

Something Gained: A Romantic Comedy Book 1
Something Earned: A Romantic Comedy Book 2

Pierce Motors

Refuel:(Pierce Motors Book l)
Pressure:(Pierce Motors Book 2)

Summer Break

Summer Nights(Summer Break Book 1)

TN Seal Security

Aydin: Book 1
Nasir: Book 2
Nicco: Book 3

Standalones

Until Serena(HEA World Novel)
Temptation
She's All I Need

I Deserve His Love
Mutual Agreement
Scoring with Sadie
Exposed (A Bodyguard Novel)
Love Shorts:A Collection of Short Stories
Red Light District(A Fantasy Romance Short)

<u>By Keke Renée:</u>
Wet Heat
His Peace, Her Pleasure
Baby, It's Cold Outside
Love Don't Live Here Anymore, Book 1, 2
Every Time We Touch (A Wet Heat Novelette)
One Night Only- Love By Design Book 1
Cassian and Savannah Love By Design Book 2
Deidra's Love -Love By Design Book 3
Protecting Bria: Book 1
Protecting Chanel:Book 2
Protecting Yanira: Book 3
Haven: A Single Dad Romance
Sensual
Seek to Please: Book 1
Seek To Touch: Book 2
Seek To Bare:Book 3
Seek To Love: Book 4
Seek To Trust: Book 5
Seek To Earn: Book 6
Tease Me: Book 1
Promise Me: Book 1

<u>By Ava S.King</u>
Fatal Memory: Book 1 Teagan Stone
Fatal Target: Book 2 Teagan Stone

Fatal Crime: Book 3 Teagan Stone
Fatal Justice: Book 4 Teagan Stone
Fatal Enemy: Book 5 Teagan Stone
Fatal Death: Book 6 Teagan Stone
Fatal Revenge: Book 7 Teagan Stone
Fatal Pursuit: Book 8 Teagan Stone
Mirror of Lies: Book 1
Mirror of Lust: Book 2
Ruined: Andi Easton Book 1

Thank you so much for reading and if you enjoyed the crazy ride and decide to leave a review we'd truly appreciate the support..

Struck of Love Universe

The Early Years-A Prequel
https://books2read.com/u/49Zjnw
Ruthless Struck In Love Book 1
https://books2read.com/u/4AxKL0
Savage Struck In Love Book 2
https://books2read.com/u/bpED6g
Beast Struck In Love Book 3
https://books2read.com/u/3LpgdJ
Janice and Carlo Captivated By His Love
https://books2read.com/u/b6je6M
Brutal Struck In Love Book 4
https://books2read.com/u/4NQyE9
Stolen-Fuertes Mafia Cartel Book 1
https://books2read.com/u/mvZlgV
Saved-Fuertes Mafia Cartel Book 2
https://books2read.com/u/4DWwLd
Redemption Struck In Love Book 5
https://books2read.com/u/b5kZ8O
Betrayal- Fuertes Mafia Cartel Book 3
https://books2read.com/u/4A5LGp

Torn: The Carrington Cartel Book 1
https://books2read.com/u/mqXare?utm_source=
universal+link
Claim: The Carrington Cartel Book 2
https://books2read.com/u/bwyjPY

About the Author

Chiquita Dennie is an author of Contemporary, Romantic Suspense, Erotic, and Women's Fiction.

Chiquita lives in Los Angeles, CA. Before she started writing contemporary romance, she worked in the entertainment industry on notable TV shows such as the Dr. Phil show, the Tyra Banks show, American Idol, and Deal or No Deal. But her favorite job is the one she's now doing: full-time writing romance.

A best-selling author and award-winning filmmaker, her first short film, "Invisible," was released in summer 2017 and screened in multiple festivals and won for Best Short Film. She also hosts a podcast that showcases the latest in beauty, business, and community called "Moscato and Tea." Her debut release of *Antonio and Sabrina Struck in Love* has opened a new avenue of writing that she loves. Nominated for 2021 Author of the Year, Best Black Romance "Mutual Agreement," and Best Interracial Romance for "She's All In Need". In 2022 nominated Author Queen of the Year, Best Black Romance "Nasir" Best Interracial Romance "Torn" and Best Romantic Comedy "Something Gained" by Black Girls Who Write.

If you want to know when the next book will come out, please visit my website at http://www.chiquitaden nie.com, where you can sign up to receive an email for my next release.

What's Next?

Want to know what happens next?

Follow me on social media to catch the next release.

Reviews are the lifeblood of the publishing world. They're read, appreciated, and needed. Please consider taking the time to leave a few words on Goodreads, or bookbub.

Sign up for updates and sneak peaks at the site below.

https://www.bookbub.com/chiquitadennie

https://www.chiquitadennie.com

https://www.goodreads.com/author/chiquitadennie

https://Facebook.com/chiquitassteamyreadinggroup

x.com/authorchiquitad

https://www.instagram.com/authorchiquitadennie

https://www.Facebook.com/authorchiquitadennie

https://www.304publishing.tumblr.com

304 Publishing Company

We showcase authors writing Romance, Women's Fiction, Thriller, and Erotic.Along with Mystery, Suspense, Poetry, Beauty, and Style Books. Thank you for taking the time out to visit. Join our mailing list to stay updated with new releases and blog posts.

www.ingramcontent.com/pod-product-compliance
Lightning Source LLC
Chambersburg PA
CBHW061242210726